BLACK-EYE CLUB

CLUB

James True

Dedicated to my patrons

CHAPTER ONE

Linus

As a boy, Linus found comfort in being invisible. He did better than others who came through a foster home. He earned a hardship pass into MIT, where he was expected to be bright and charming. That was before the ethics violations. Linus' morality suffered from autism. During the first week of labs, he ostracized himself over the difference between a lab rat and a dog from the pound. His social credit finally tanked after he wired the copper pipes in the girl's dorm with an acoustic thumper. The sonic device pounded a subliminal rhythm into every bathroom and water fountain. He presented his findings to the department advisor, documenting several changes in resident behavior with charts tracking dorm-room sleep patterns and facial analysis. It was stunning to watch all that earnestness converted to wincing. The advisor called the Provost for support. The campus had already reported a spike in pregnancy, and parents would soon have their reason. The legal solution was to delegitimize the incident with a statement by the campus police that read, "Incident of vandalism by a bipolar schizophrenic perpetrating a voyeuristic fantasy to cope with the pressures of school."

Not everyone was offended by Linus' actions. He was invited to Buffalo to work under a psychotherapist as a sound healer. He installed his acoustic stimulator inside a therapy couch in the basement and bolted the unit to the floor. He explained how it worked to a new client, Rose, "The spine is a harp. Each vertebra is a string you pluck with the right tone. The pelvis gets three orbiting arpeggios. The lumber likes two." Rose wanted to know if what she heard was true, and forty minutes later, she was groaning its merits through the door. She told Linus, "I see a lucrative career up a never-ending ladder of unsatisfied housewives." Linus felt awkward, but Rose said, "Stop that. My husband owes me. Besides, this thing works!" Linus saw his technology ruin him as a romantic, but he could not look back. For the first time in his life, he was good at something.

There was a stern banging on the door. Linus heard his landlord orating a declaration from the stairs. He listed the reasons Linus had to move out of the building. Rose laughed and said, "Come to Africa. Stay with me for a while." Rose caressed the chair, "Bring your new invention."

CHAPTER TWO

Leda

Linus met Leda on the jet sent from Africa. She buckled herself into the harness of the galley's rumble seat facing him. Linus could not help but gawk. Leda did not change her pace. She understood the energy of being seen. Their eyes connected as wheels barreled down the tarmac. Their unbroken stare convinced gravity to lift them from the runway and leave Miami's shore. Leda was not smitten with Linus; she was mesmerized by his peculiarity. His aura tasted of power and pity. After the craft leveled, the copilot opened the door and exclaimed, "Leda! What are you doing here?" Linus watched her face light up as she unbuckled. She crawled inside the cockpit and closed the door, saying, "Hi stranger!"

Gender abnormalities appear in as much as five percent of the population, but fewer than five hundred true hermaphrodites have been documented in modern history. Linus didn't know it, but Leda was one of them. The hermaphrodite is not a mutation. As many as 94% of plants that flower are just like Leda. A true hermaphrodite has functioning ovaries and testicles. Leda has eight fully functioning glandular dimensions, while Linus only has seven. People like Linus sense this lack when Leda is present. Like them, he can't place it, and it makes him mad.

Leda had suffered from epilepsy. Nine years ago, the seizures were so frequent they performed a craniotomy. Leda spent her twelfth birthday listening to a bone saw cut into her cranial vault like a tomb. Doctors opened her head and installed 85 subdural electrodes along her brain's cortical surface. Once open, a two-centimeter area of the superior frontal gyrus was stimulated with electricity, and Leda giggled. The voltage stopped, and Leda was asked how she felt, and she said, "You're funny." The doctor applied more voltage this time, and Leda laughed even harder. They asked Leda why she was laughing, and she said, "You guys are just so funny standing around like that."

For three months, they stood around waiting for Leda to have a seizure, but it never came. As the fiscal quarter closed, they added a new specialist to the team. Dr. Blueman brought with him a deeper motivation for answers. Leda had a seizure two days later. Her second came two days after that. The team was nearly unanimous in recommending resective surgery. It was Dr Blueman who suggested the radical idea of giving Leda an engineered strain of rabies.

The Rabies virus is shaped like a bullet. A single infected neuron can destroy the entire brain in days. It has devastating effects on memory that go unnoticed as the central nervous system boils the body alive. Dr. Blueman could control the virus if the injection entered the hippocampus. He believed this would stop the seizures without surgery. He was right. The orphanage had confidence in Dr. Blueman and sent Leda to his private treatment center, Shamba Macho.

CHAPTER THREE

Shamba

On a private airfield in Africa, a jeep and a motorcycle arrive from opposite directions. The drivers, both game wardens, nod to each other in unison and converse as they wait. They are identical twins in every way except rank. The jet lands and taxis its way back up the runway. Leda jumps out to embrace the man on the motorcycle. She climbs onto his back, and the two drive away before Linus can leave the plane. His face betrays disappointment at her leaving. The driver helps Linus load his trunk into the jeep and laughs, "I see you met, Leda?" Linus nodded and pointed to the motorcycle speeding away, "Who's that?" The driver smirked, "That is Tombo."

As they drove to the shamba, Linus' mood improved. He sunk into the landscape of Tanzania. Its somber flatlands gave every plain a sense of nowhere. Linus made small talk, "Do you work at the ranch?" The man nodded and explained, "My brothers and I are rangers. We hunt poachers for Buddy." Linus noticed the rifle cage behind him and realized these guns were for shooting people. He introduced himself to the driver, "My name's Linus, and I am not a poacher." The driver laughed and said, "Yes, I can see that." Linus' attention was riding on the back of a motorcycle two kilometers south.

Botswana is in the center of Africa's lower ventricle. From here, we trace the oldest DNA squeezed from the black sediment. The ancient name of Africa is Alkebulan. This name means "Land of the Blacks" by the Ethiopians. In Hebrew, the word denotes the "mother of mankind" or "garden of Eden." Alkebulan is Arabic, derived from the root "qabl," meaning "the ones before." All of these names reference a land of endless forgetting. Alkebulan is the antithesis of the sun. She swallows it all in her forgetful sand. Only in the pit of mystery could the earth give birth to awareness. The word sapiens means awareness. Homo sapiens sapiens is man's awareness of his awareness.

Rose greeted Linus in the driveway and was delighted to see him. "You came!" She said as if she was surprised. Linus knew she couldn't have been surprised. Rose brought him inside and doted over everything she had done to prepare his quarters. She told him, "Take a few days to recover from the flight. Make yourself at home." Linus stopped her, "Give me an hour to unpack my couch, and we'll do a quick session?" A belt of exuberance cried out in the halls as Rose declared, "Do you hear that world? Linus Bardo is going to spoil me!"

After a noisy session, Rose laid down for a nap. Linus gave himself a tour of the property. He saw a boy throwing a baseball with another older boy. The boys were identical in every way except in age and length. It was so stunning Linus could not help but gawk. In unison, the duo stopped and glared at him. They were as human as Linus, but he felt his body on high alert. Linus had never encountered a wild animal with so much intelligence. The cortisol dried his mouth out, and his stance went numb. He froze until a voice behind him broke the spell, "Afternoon, Finn." Finn waved in perfect sync and answered, "Hi, Buddy."

Buddy asked Linus, "So you're the massage guy from Buffalo who's come to satisfy my wife?" Linus sweated out an answer, "My machine satisfies her. — Er. I mean, the machine generates an acoustic scalar wave to stimulate her vagus nerve satisfactorily." Linus was hyperventilating. Buddy laughed and eased his spirits, "I'm just messing with you sport. You and I share a common interest. If Rose is happy, you and I are happy. "After years of trying, Rose and Buddy abandoned having children. It ruined the intimacy, and Linus' chair seemed to help. Buddy understood the threat of poachers, but Linus wasn't a concern. Before Rose, Buddy was a bankrupt veterinarian living on a sailboat. He was hired on her family's ranch, and the two eloped. Rose turned Buddy around, and he was running the business a few years later.

Buddy put Linus into his truck and took him for a drive around the shamba. Once out of view, Linus told Buddy, "I embarrassed myself back in the garden. I wanted to apologize, but I froze up." Buddy assured Linus, "That reaction is normal when you meet Finn."

Coming over the hill, Buddy saw a motorcycle parked next to the river bank. He pulled up next to it and whistled from the cab. The engine was still running, and Linus thought about what to say next. Buddy whistled again but didn't get a response. Linus interjected, "I don't think he's alone." Buddy's brow curled in confusion. Linus explained, "A woman was on the plane. First, she was in the cockpit. Then she was on a motorcycle." Linus pointed at the bike. Buddy's curiosity creased into strain as he said, "Leda." He dropped the transmission into gear and spun out in the dust.

Leda was straddling Tombo on a picnic table by the river when she heard Buddy's whistle. She shoved her boob in Tombo's mouth and said, "Be quiet." They listened childishly to see if they were in trouble. The heavy breathing created an atmosphere, and Tombo was erupting. Buddy whistled again, and Tombo started to tell him off. Leda begged him, "No.

Don't. You will only make it harder for me." Tombo implored her, "Leda. Why do you let them milk you like a goat?" Leda pushed Tombo down and teased him, "But, Tombo? You milk me like a goat."

Following the river, as they drove, Linus saw the ghost of a beast grazing on the other side and pointed enthusiastically, "Is that an albino rhino?" Buddy nodded. Linus saw his spirit had degraded and tried to help, "Your place is beautiful." Buddy nodded again and explained, "It isn't ours. We curate the museum, and they let us do what we want. Our ranch is in Virginia."

Linus asked, "The twins in the garden? They are part of the museum?" Buddy corrected him, "Not twins. Identicals. And yes, they are part of the collection." Linus asked, "Is this a slave farm?" Buddy was mildly insulted, "Our crop has contracts in their chromosomes. They made a blood oath to be archived, mutated, planted, and harvested at the museum's discretion." Linus said, "Who would do that?" and Buddy replied, "Women donate eggs all the time. $50,000 if the genes are right." Buddy went on, "But not everyone does it for money. People like believing they could live forever in a genetic library. It makes them feel important." Linus thought about why people buy tombstones. Buddy was catering to this desire on a million-dollar level.

Linus asked, "How do you install a contract inside someone's chromosome?" Buddy replied, "A lawyer pricks your finger, and you declare a contract under oath. The injury creates a marker the charter can use to deposition your intent in court." Linus asked Buddy, "Is this how the Finns joined the farm?" Buddy nodded and answered, "You need three generations to consent. All of them were on the mother's side. When you satisfy that, all future generations are under contract at birth until confirmation." Linus repeated to him, "Confirmation?" Buddy nodded, "One is confirmed by proving they can write to their chromosomes. Once confirmed, you become the custodian of your family's contract and can make amendments."

Linus was puzzled, "How do you amend a chromosome? Is this an oath, or do you edit your genes?" Buddy replied, "No difference. Everything you say is written in your nucleotides. It's just a matter of finding them. Every couple of hours, your RNA makes a copy of your genes somewhere. That copy has every mutation you made stored in its record." Linus was considering his genes. Buddy said, "Every nasty word you've ever said. Every lie you've ever told. Every person you've cursed is somewhere in there."

Buddy pointed at the rhino and said, "That fella's horn is $60,000 a kilo in Vietnam. That's all it is — one big toenail growing on his nose. You and I throw our fingernail clippings in the trash. Makes you wonder why there's not a market for human toenails?" Linus chided, "Maybe there is?" Before they left, Linus asked Buddy, "How'd you make him white?" Buddy joked, "Lots and lots of practice."

After the tour, Linus found Rose in the stable, tending to a pair of black horses. Linus asked, "Are they clones?" Rose smiled and answered, "They are identicals. This one is Castor, and that's Pollux." Linus wondered, "How do you know who is who?" Rose answered, "It can be harder to tell with these two, but their markings are distinct." Linus nervously asked the horses, " Which of you is in charge?" Rose replied, "That would be me."

Linus made it uncomfortable by asking, "There was a woman on the plane. The pilot called her Leda?" Rose's face dropped, "Oh Fuck. What did she do?" Linus laughed in surprise, "Nothing. No. It's just that Buddy was telling me about your museum, and I wanted to know if she was part of the collection?" Rose conveyed her annoyance as she answered, "No." She led the stallions into the arena, with

Linus following. He noticed how they seemed to twitch in unison. Like the Finns, they were completely in sync. Linus focused on his goal, "So she's not a clone?" Rose replied, "No. Leda is not identical. She is a surrogate contractor." Linus noticed how annoyed Rose was. She took a deep breath and said, "Leda works with Dr. Blueman. That's all." Rose's answer was truthful and dishonest.

Linus tried to regain his composure and pointed to the stallions, "What makes them twitch in unison like that?" Rose answered, "I say quantum entanglement. Buddy says it's epigenetics. No one knows, really. Memories from the original are installed in each identical. It's strange to watch. These two have never trained for dressage, yet their transitions are perfect. I can't tell the difference between them. I correct one, and the other seems to know it from inside the barn."

Linus shook his head, "That's impossible." Rose said, "That's what Buddy said, but I don't care what you boys think is possible. I've bred horses my whole life, and cloning makes strange foals. Their hormones are already activated. They are born with a gender that's already informed. A lot of memories are pre-installed before they were born. We can't keep them in the same paddock as other foals. They are fully developed and ready to fight or mate. Buddy cloned a gelding last year, and the owner noticed it carried the same fear of garden hoses as its donor." Linus was fascinated, "Wow. So that fear is somewhere in the DNA?" Rose retorted, "Maybe. Blueman said all clones share the same quantum."

Linus said, "It must be terrifying to be afraid of something that never happened or be motivated by something that never even inspired you initially." Rose agreed, "These two are physically healthy, but spiritually, they are haunted by things that never occurred." Linus replied, "Sounds like Hell." Rose confirmed as she stroked Castor, "I told Buddy no more clones. He told me I needed to relax." Linus smirked, "Well, it's a good thing I'm here."

CHAPTER FOUR

Vulture

Africa is a wild, latent space. It is home to the world's deadliest predators, among which are Homo sapiens. A collection of rhinos is called a crash, and a collection of people is called a civilization. Tombo lacked the folly of distinguishing man from beast. He, like Africa, understood them all as one big reef. Every man with a name is striving to become his own species. Until then, he must civilize under the authority of herd instinct. Sovereignty is a place civilization can never afford to reach.

Many recorded cases have occurred of people raised in the wild and failing to return to society. The transition proved impossible because the refugees could not navigate the human race. Nature's deceptions are elementary by comparison. A civilized predator raises your family before it turns you into meat. Wildlings fail to acclimate and retreat to the safety of a cave. The simplicity of a brutal winter is favorable to a tribe of smiling teeth.

Thanks to Shamba Macho, Tombo was a giraffe among hyenas. He was hired as a game warden before Buddy and Rose arrived from the States. Vibe is the alchemy of geography, and Tombo knew his territory. His first encounter at the shamba happened in the early afternoon. He was alone, thirty kilometers south of the perimeter. Tombo maneuvered himself behind some trees to surprise two suspected poachers. He came from behind and ordered them with his rifle, "Howzit! Up! Up!" The men raised their hands as high as possible, which wasn't much. They were caked in rotting wildebeest and draped in a robe of flies. Their armpits seemed to shine like the sun. One of them held the neck of a limp vulture. Its freshly plucked eyes had been harvested in a bottle to see the future. Tombo pointed to the eyes in the jar and scolded them, asking, "Why did you not see me coming?"

The men did not speak. They lacked the skills to practice language under pressure. A twitch was all it took to set them free. Each bolted like a gazelle in opposite directions. Instinct rejects patience and comradery. These things are functions of memory. Instinct only knows how to run away. Conscience is an expensive thing because self-rebuke requires reflection. Self-reflection is scarce because ignorance is a skill in the Serengeti. It gave these men more options than Tombo.

CHAPTER FIVE

Hyena

Man climbs Africa's cradle on a trellis of slavery. He uses its rungs to reach new vistas of sovereignty. Slaves are men who still crawl. A worker is a boss who still grovels. When the hyena finds shame, he becomes a giraffe. When the giraffe finds courage, he becomes a lion. When the lion finds love, he becomes an elephant. When the elephant finds God, he becomes a man.

The Germans colonized the Tanzanian coast in 1885, and everything changed. An electric fence of civilization surrounded Africa. Private property has never existed in Tanzania. The concept is psychotic because no one can hold territory without presence. Hegemony changed the rules of Africa by raising the bar on success. This new threshold destroyed many and helped a few.

Zuri remembers the thud on the kitchen table. Yared served them a duffel bag stuffed with money. It was fatter than a turkey and steamy from the dust and filth. Yared was sweating through broken teeth, waiting for his family to smile. The room was speechless. Zuri spoke for everyone when she demanded, "What have you done?" Yared tasted her insolence in the alkaline of his saliva.

He laughed when he answered, saying, "Nothing." The hyena is innocent until proven guilty. He speaks sarcasm to ensure his words are meaningless. There was no blood on Yared's hands. All his fingers touched were money. In six hours, Yared earned more than his entire village could make in a lifetime. All he had to do was look away.

Yared worked security at the preserve. The team infiltrated the compound after he unlocked the gate. A team of hunters used darts to tranquilize the rhino and collected its horn in the dark. When Yared heard their chainsaw, he told himself it was a motorcycle. Zuri extracted Yared's confession by eviscerating his deniability. The final excuse came when he claimed they would have done it anyway. Zuri scolded him, "You have shamed us, Yared." Yared said the worst thing he could, "I did this for you, Zuri."

Zuri needed more than money to swallow what her father had done. Growing up under his roof had always been a struggle. Yared had learned to profit from his lack of conscience. People came to know him as a man who could be trusted to do something wrong. He had been this way for as long as she could remember, and his strategy had finally paid off. Yared was morally bankrupt. He had liquidated all of his assets into a bag of paper currency. It takes 570 Somali shillings to equal one U.S. Dollar. The inflation grows higher every day.

Swahili's language changes as you move across the continent. The words are gentler in the Tanzanian heartland, where it is expected to be soft and humble. In Tanzanian Swahili, you pray if you can ask someone a question. In Kenyan Swahili, this is weak and confusing. Words dehydrate as you move into Somalia. The Horn of Africa is a brutal place. The salination is so high the land's water conducts electricity. Zuri banished Yared as she screamed, "Get out! Go back to Somalia with your innocence."

In Vietnam, when someone is dying, the only thing more important than saving them is proving you did your best. This is the only medicinal ingredient in rhino horn. Its powder doesn't save the sick; it saves the sick's family from feeling guilty. The rhino horn is a medicine for them. Shortly after her father was banished, Zuri signed a contract as a gestational surrogate for the museum. She carried one of Tombo's embryos and gave birth in a hospital. She never saw it again. Like her father, she, too, came home with a bag of money. Tombo's crop had eighteen gestational surrogate workers in total. Zuri was one of the three who delivered successfully.

CHAPTER SIX

Hatch

When Leda first came to Shamba Macho, she was a shy and reserved little girl. The ranch gave her two years without a seizure. She helped around the ranch and was always willing to work in the stables. Back home, Leda was a celebrity in the medical community. Her journey back from epilepsy brought in a substantial donation to the orphanage. Leda never complained and always wore a smile during interviews. At the request of Dr. Blueman, the state of Nigeria approved the orphanage's petition to emancipate Leda at the age of fourteen. They agreed Leda's long-term care could suffer under the limitations of governmental approval.

Dr. Blueman was concerned the seizure would return as Leda's brain continued to grow. He offered Leda room, board, and a lifetime of treatment if she donated her eggs to science. He told her being a hermaphrodite made her eggs special. Leda could not understand because she had always considered herself a monster. Leda agreed and began a regiment of hormones. Her ovaries were mined for three years under the supervision of Buddy and Rose. In that time, Leda produced sixty-six eggs in four harvests. The fifth harvest didn't happen because Leda missed her period.

There was no one in the house to save Leda. There was nowhere for her to hide. Her spine was cornered in the chair at the dining room table, and Rose was the inquisition. Leda swore she was a virgin as she clutched her womb, insisting, "Bikira!" She seemed just as perplexed as Rose. Rose wasn't angry at Leda. She was angry at God. Rose told herself she was professionally offended as a breeder. Rose and Buddy treated Leda like family and showed her more respect than all of the museum's residents. She slept in their home and ate at their table. To make the pain worse, Leda had something Rose lacked — fertility.

Rose berated her in the chair, "Tell me, Leda! Who?!" For the first time since coming to the ranch, Leda entered the threshold of a seizure. This is a tangible place where the first clouds of the brain's electrical storm form in the outside world. Leda felt a pounding sense of deja vu as the brain overwhelmed itself with processing. Consciousness is a criticality where the brain's hemispheres find unity. We see this phenomenon in the stadium when a crowd erupts in a harmonious wave. The egregore has recognized itself in the criticality. This identity is gestalt erupting from a Goldilocks zone.

Leda's egregore was panicking, and she wanted it to stop. To free herself, she pointed at Buddy, "Him. It was him. Is that what you wanted to hear?" Rose turned to see Buddy standing behind her. He froze in the headlights of the accusation. Rose smelled guilt all over him. Buddy gathered as much shame as he could from her brow and took it out of the house. Rose followed him outside to give more from the tack room. When they came out, Leda had run away.

Tombo found Leda five days later in a ranger outpost fifteen kilometers away. He stuck his head inside the door and called, "Tunda?" Leda recognized his voice and crawled out of a cabinet to reveal herself. Tombo had noticed the lions showing interest in the abandoned hut like never before. They had caught the smell of a fugitive inside. Tombo was moved by the fact Leda wasn't mauled. He spoke to the cats in Swahili, thanking them for their protection. He squatted beside her on the hut's dirt floor and gave her water and a sandwich. She curled up in Tombo's chest and ate. The lion preserve wasn't a place you walked through alone. Tombo recognized this as a very special omen for Leda.

The sun dove into the horizon, and Tombo told Leda, "Let's take you home." Leda shook her head and begged, "Please don't." Tombo asked, "You want to join me on patrol?" Leda smiled, and he loaded her onto his motorcycle. The pair made it safely to the southern perimeter and parked. Tombo was more cautious than usual with his cargo. The perimeter is dangerous, and poachers aren't the only threat he needed to watch out for. Leda was gazing up at the stars. She asked Tombo which was his favorite, and he told her he could never choose. He said, "The Karanga say stars are the eyes of the dead. The Tswana say it is those who are afraid to be born. Either way, how do you tell one it's your favorite while all the others look at you?" Leda thought about it and said, "I guess you have to whisper."

Protecting the preserve from poachers was a full-time job, especially during the new moon when it was so dark. The shamba was far too big and impractical to fence, and walls would only cripple its residence. The only solution was Tombo and his brothers. There are three types of game wardens in Africa, and the smallest percentage of them are certified by a government agency. The industry is a mix between privateers who love Africa and the people who lack luxury for such feelings.

Tombo parked under a tree stand on the eastern border and hoisted Leda onto his shoulders so she could push herself through the floor's hatch. The two sat for hours listening to the grass swirl in the breeze. Tombo told stories about the stars with his mouth covered with a bandana. Leda asked why she had to cover her mouth when she spoke, and Tombo told her, "So the animals won't see."

The receptors in Leda's brain were hungry for meat, and the smell of Tombo only teased them. There is no concept of addiction when you are permanently dilated. This was Leda's normal. She slurped electricity from the room regardless of what it took to drink. She leaned in and bit Tombo on the neck. Tombo told her to stop, but Leda ignored him. She wrapped her haunches around Tombo's frame and climbed him like a tree. Tombo dropped his rifle and said, "Quiet girl. You will bring the lions to us." It was too late. Leda's mane was erect. Tombo heard her righteousness command, "Take me, or I will scream."

Constellations reflect what we want more than they reflect who we are. The star Regulus sits in the chest of the constellation Leo. The Lion rules the transition from Cancer to Virgo. Leo's power renews death with a harvest from his kingdom's virginity. Regulus is the celestial doorway for the luminaries to bless the newborn king. The Persians called this Shir. The Turks called it Artan. The Syrians called it Aryo. The Jews called it Arye. The Indians called it Simha. Egyptians associated the Lion with Anubis because of this journey through the underworld. The Lion was a crucial part of the renewal and the scientific principles of cellular death; Apophis is named for this Lion's gate. All of these cultures relate the Lion to Regulus except one. That country is Africa. In Africa, Regulus is known as the wildebeest.

The wildebeest is a willing beast. It finds worth in feeding Africa's royalty. Timing a kill is everything to a king. The royalty of position requires it to be necessary and clean. Cortisol from a messy kill spoils every cut of meat and turns the process into a death instead of a harvest. The word

Tabernacle means "the very best offering of meat." The Lion does not kill; it resurrects. He ends all life it deems decrepit to make room for new growth. It prunes the land, making room for its bounty. This is in the heart of Regulus.

Tombo brought Leda home the following afternoon. Rose embraced her in the driveway and scanned her face, asking if she was okay. Buddy came home that night to Leda sitting at the dining room table where he last saw her. Neither Leda nor Rose would acknowledge Buddy in the room. He never got to ask what happened. Tombo told Buddy where he found her and how it was a miracle the lions didn't take her.

CHAPTER SEVEN

Dinner

Five years had passed, and the dining room still hadn't changed. Rose began the evening meal by announcing, "Mr Blueman expressed his regrets about not joining us and looks forward to meeting you, Linus." Linus saw his empty chair and had his first mystery solved. After they sat down, Leda came into the house calling out, "Dr. Blueman?" Rose and Buddy froze in place, trying not to make a sound, but Linus caved and gave away their coordinates, "He's not here." Leda came into the dining room and exclaimed, "What's this? A plot to dine without me?" Rose squirmed in her chair before relenting. She pointed to Blueman's seat, and told her, "You're welcome to join us."

   Buddy greeted Leda, "Back so soon?" Leda pointed to her loins and announced, "The Stargate is open for business." Leda landed in Blueman's seat and sniffed at Linus, asking, "Did they tell you about me?" Before Linus could answer, a little girl rushed in and took command of the room, "What about you, Mommy?" Everyone dropped their guard. The little girl climbed up and swallowed Leda's face like a monster. Leda kissed her daughter affectionately, saying, "My little Tunda."

Linus had long carried the gift of being awkward, but he was no match for Leda. She was a neon panther in human skin. Linus was dining with something more advanced than himself, giving him a hollow feeling he never knew. Want is the cry for expansion. We expand from this lack. The darkness despised Leda because light could not be ignored. Her presence revealed what was missing, and people wanted Leda to suffer for showing this to them.

Leda asked Linus, "Are you here for long?" Linus answered, "I thought I'd work through the dry season. Or as long as Rose and Buddy will have me." Rose replied, "It is a pleasure to have you, Mr. Bardo." Buddy was quieter than usual. He held a knife over a sweet potato as if something was about to happen. Leda congratulated Linus, "Everyone can hear how good you are at what you do." Buddy interjected, "Knock it off, Leda." Leda was bewildered, "Who? Me? Or them?" Linus showed some courage, "The chair is designed to stimulate different bones and nerves in the body. You should try it sometime. It might bring you some relief." Buddy tacked a different course for the table, "Finn said someone was snooping around Blueman's lab last week. All of you keep your ears open." Rose said jeeringly, "Tombo seems to be distracted lately. Maybe we should hire someone to help out with security." Leda spits back, "Well, maybe Tombo could hear better if you weren't so loud at moaning."

Lyra asked Rose, "Can I go play in the closet?" Leda stood up and answered for her, "Of course, Tunda. Go pick us out something to wear, eh? I want to say one last thing." Everyone at the table watched Lyra squeal with joy up the stairs. Leda asked Linus, "Did you know Buddy has a chair like yours?" Linus gulped and shook his head as he said, "No." Leda told Linus, "Ask him." Linus looked at Buddy frozen in his chair. Leda said to Buddy, "Tell him about the time you strapped me into it." Buddy was a statue. Leda leaned into his ear and said, "Remember? I was blind! Remember?" Leda quoted Buddy's words to him, "It's time to be brave, Leda!" Linus was petrified. Buddy answered bitterly, "Funny. You don't look blind to me."

CHAPTER EIGHT

Cave

Leda was fourteen when she sat in the chair, and Buddy told her, "It's time to be brave." She nodded and sank her teeth into the mouthguard as her legs were cinched into their harness. The blood pressure sleeve squeezed her arm and made her fingers tingle. The chair hissed like a rocket as it leaned back into the launch position. Blueman strapped her headpiece to the chair and told her, "Sit tight. We need a few minutes to calibrate."

Leda wriggled like a bug on a pin. She wondered if this was what calibration felt like. The melodrama from the stain in the ceiling was over when Blueman rolled into Leda's viewport. His hairy arms looked like a giant insect stuffed with meat. Its finger pressed the record button and spoke with authority, "Patient BEC-LV3. Age fourteen. The subject is left-handed." Buddy nodded to confirm, but Blueman wasn't looking. "Beginning the first injection." A moist cotton ball blotted Leda's upper right cheek, and the vapor teared up in her eye. Blueman revealed the long needle required for para-retinal delivery. Leda stared down its steel barrel as Blueman plunged his way into her cornea. It reached the bottom of a vitreous ocean and buried its black payload into the soil of her retina. Leda heard Buddy say, "Good girl," as her eye sank into a black sea. Blueman recorded Leda's pupils into the record, "Mydriasis six millimeters right. Two millimeters left. Preparing second injection." Leda's heart sank as she considered what was coming.

Blueman asked Buddy, "Close the door and pull the curtains, please." Blueman dissolved 0.2 grams of white crystal methamphetamine in 0.2 milliliters of water and filled the syringe. He returned to Leda's side, wrapped a rubber tourniquet around her elbow, and spoke to the recorder," Lighting the cave." His needle found the pipeline in her elbow and dropped a match into its vein. Blueman rolled his chair across the room, turned off the lights, and said, "Welcome to Hades."

Leda heard a whisper a thousand miles away tell her, "We are coming for you." She felt the regiment of spiders descend from the walls of her cranium and jab their hairy mandibles into her brain. Electric eels swarmed the reef of her backbone, burrowing into the cracks in her vertebrae. Leda was boiling in cranial fluid as she heard Blueman explain, "What we see inside the retina is an agreement between our senses and what we are willing to face." All Leda could hear was her heart screaming. It wanted out of its ribcage. She spit out her mouthpiece and gasped, "Let me out." Blueman understood the importance of this moment and denied her request. He continued to explain calmly, "Dopamine is the gasoline of vision. The eyes are lubricated in its butter. Without dopamine, the eyes don't function. This is how the amygdala stops a system crash." As if possessed, Leda's assemblage flipped as she started laughing hysterically, "How do I stop this? Is there a button somewhere?"

Blueman was relieved by Leda's laughter. He had never administered the serum to a child. Leda was the youngest member of the Black-Eye Club, and he didn't know how she would handle the front-row seat. In the land of the blind, the one-eyed man cries because no one relates to what he sees. Leda's brain melted into its new assembly. Blueman encouraged her to relax and let the hallucination run uninhibited. Blueman heard Leda crying in the dark and noticed Buddy was crying, too. Blueman told him, "Estrogen-rich tears activate testosterone production in a man's body. Emotional tears secrete a much higher protein concentration than the eye's regular lubrication. Crying is one of the most effective ways to teleport emotion." Buddy believed him and said, "I can tell."

In the darkness, Blueman explained the importance of immobilizing Leda during installation, "The face is a joystick into the emotional body. It corrupts the serum's effectiveness to have facial contact because she can regulate off us and dampen its effects." Buddy was struck with compassion for Leda, "How does this help with the seizures?" Blueman answered, "It dilates the opening of her mind enough to reveal the daemon." Buddy had never heard Blueman say that term, "Demons?" Blueman replied, "Daemons. A daemon is an application launched in the background without a user present."

Buddy asked, "Like a virus?" Blueman said, "If you don't claim your own body, you might call them viruses. But it would be more accurate to call them abandoned intent. Once the arrow of intention leaves the bow, it becomes a vectored will. Even if the archer changes his intention, it is too late. The arrow is already on its way to the target."

Buddy asked, "So everyone is possessed?" Blueman answered, "Raw psychic intent is released from your breath whenever you speak. You can't turn this off. It comes from the blood that evaporates when you work with your hands. Will is converted into a chemosignal inside the heart and installed in each blood cell that enters its chambers." Buddy said, "So I can smell your will?" Blueman answered, "Yes, but the olfactory equipment in the roof of your mouth shuts down after you are born, so it's not obvious. If it was, it might possess you completely. Smells are electrical fields. These fields reprogram the electric brain. The smell is rendered emotionally when we look at someone through our retina. We sense, or smell, someone's intention in their vibration." Buddy said, "Horses are intuitive. Their olfactory gland is six times as powerful as yours and mine. Do they see demons?" Blueman nodded, "Sounds like it. The olfactory decodes sex, age, fertility, vigor, and intention all from scent. The more we understand the link between will and scent, the more words like daemons, hauntings, and possessions seem to fit. Leda's epilepsy is an electrical possession. Once she sees this daemon, the pheromones that haunt her will stop. All she lacks is the integration of displaced electricity."

That night, Buddy brought Leda ice cream, but she didn't want to eat. Buddy asked if she was in pain, and Leda answered, "My eye doesn't hurt, but everything tastes blue." Buddy wondered if this was normal, but before he could respond, she said," Blue tastes like rubber." She exclaimed as she joked, "Listen to the flavor as I say it slowly — Bah-loo. Can you taste that?"

The following morning, Leda went to open her eyes, but nothing happened. All she pinged was blue. She cried out frantically, but it didn't seem to penetrate. It felt like a blanket of nothing. She believed she could move but lacked a destination to motivate. She jolted when a hand grabbed her. She sensed a shadowy blue matchstick rattling fear from its head until she cried out for it to stop. A heartbeat began to pound over a loudspeaker. A gust of stress slapped her in the face that felt like Rose. Leda saw pulses of emotion bouncing against the furniture of a blue room. The energy of will was all Leda could paint on her radar. Buddy seemed to be shouting at Blueman, but Leda couldn't sense him anywhere. Leda's skin grew itchy, and with a slurred tongue, she yelled, "Who are you talking to?" Blueman touched Leda on the shoulder, but she jumped again as if a ghost grabbed her. Leda didn't hear Blueman exclaim, "Look! No seizure." She didn't see him pointing at her brainwaves on the screen in celebration because Leda could not see through all the molecules in the atmosphere.

Buddy was terrified and began shaking Leda, saying her name as if she needed to wake up. But Leda wasn't asleep. Her eyes have never been this open. Her amygdala had relented, and she was seeing reality without inhibition. Blueman was the only one pleased. He knew Leda couldn't see or hear him, so he instructed Buddy, "Tell her she will be fine in a couple of hours. Her thalamus has delivered the amygdala its final ultimatum, and her hallucination can reboot."

CHAPTER NINE

Babinski

An hour later, Buddy found Blueman in the pool house and yelled through the glass, "Did you give her crystal meth?" Blueman opened the door and let Buddy in, saying, "I gave Leda three ingredients. Methamphetamine was one of them, yes." Buddy followed him, exasperating, "But. She's blind!" Blueman corrected him, "She was blind. Now she sees. She needs time to unlearn. You'll see." Buddy demanded, "What's in the serum?" Blueman answered, "The first injection inhibits melanin. The last excites dopamine. The methamphetamine stretches her aperture, amplifying the results." Buddy asked, "Aperture?" Blueman said, "Yes, the lens of consciousness through which we hallucinate." Buddy said, "Hallucinate? Are we all hallucinating now?" Blueman handed Buddy a drink and said, "Of course we are."

The men sat down, and Blueman explained, "Anton-Babinski syndrome, otherwise known as visual anosognosia, is a condition where people who cannot see insist they can. Ever heard of it?" Buddy was confused, "No. But Leda doesn't have that?" Blueman laughed, "Precisely. It is you who suffers from this affliction, not her." Buddy sat back, "But I have perfect vision." Blueman chuckled, "That's exactly what someone with Anton-Babinski syndrome would say." Buddy scolded, "This is bullshit. Do you have this syndrome, too?" Blueman replied, "I used to. But, I found the cure." Buddy said it like the idea was ridiculous, "Crystal meth cures Babinski syndrome?" Blueman ignored him, "I need you to rethink what the eyes do. They are displays for the brain. Everything your brain sent to the retina went through its filter first."

Buddy said, "But my eyes see the world, not my brain." Blueman corrected him, "Not true. Your eyes transmit data through an optic cable into the back of your head where a painting is made. That painting is projected onto your retinal wall. The wall is where you see the world." Buddy noticed, "Sounds like Plato's Cave." Blueman replied, "Precisely. The optic nerve is the entrance to this cavern. You never see the real world. We only see its shadow on the wall." Buddy asked, "So your serum shows the world outside the cave?" Blueman corrected him, "The serum brings more of the real world's shadows into our hallucination in the cave." Buddy looked at Blueman squarely and said, "I don't believe you." Blueman laughed, "That's Babinski for you."

Blueman could see that Buddy was not amused. The idea made him uncomfortable. Blueman asked Buddy, "You're the vet. Are horses color blind?" Buddy shook his head, "They are dichromatic. They see blue and green, but not red." Blueman agreed, "Red does not exist in the horse's mind?" Buddy answered, "I guess not." Blueman continued, "There are colors outside our mind, too. Like the horse, we believe we see a complete spectrum." Buddy asked, "So what colors do you see that I don't?" Blueman said, "We see the same colors, but I see them in higher resolution. The shades are more vibrant and distinct. They have a deeper emotional meaning because I see more of the color's information. I see its aura. "Buddy's face was incredulous, "You can see my aura?" Blueman nodded. Buddy asked him, "Are you high, Blueman?" Blueman said, "I see what fish and birds see. I see electricity. I see the aura of human scent. What do you want me to call it if not your aura?"

Buddy was frustrated, "I'm just used to a world where the only way the human body can choose what it sees is by turning its head." Blueman asked him, "Consider a car's speedometer. If you press the gas pedal to the floor, does that make the car travel 120 miles per hour?" Buddy said, "No. The speedometer rises as the car accelerates." Blueman said, "If you release the gas pedal, does that stop the car?" Buddy answered, "Of course not." Blueman asked, "But why not?" Buddy said, "Because of physics. Because of momentum. Because a gas pedal doesn't work like that." Blueman agreed, "Our eyes don't work like that either."

Blueman asked, "Did you know the eye can never see blue? Not directly. Blue is a hallucination from your peripheral vision. The retina's blue cones are outside the perimeter of your fovea." Buddy wasn't impressed, "So what?" Blueman explained, "Blue is a construct. It's an advanced hallucination only some of us can render in the retina. Blue is a skill man developed over time."

Buddy sucked on an ice cube as Blueman explained more, "Homer's Illiad was a story about a journey across the sea, and not once did he use the word 'blue' to describe it. Instead, he wrote the phrase' wine-eyed sea.' He does this dozens of times and uses the same term to describe the color of blood." Buddy considered, "So you're saying he didn't see blue?" Blueman asked back, "Does a horse see red?" Buddy interjected, "But horses can't see red because they don't have the cones." Blueman came back, "And you can't see blue because there are no blue cones in your fovea." Buddy joked, "This can't be right." Blueman disagreed, "You have a degree in medicine. You know the retina discerns color through its cones. But did you know that only one in fifty cones is blue receptive? If the eyes worked as you understand them, we would not see blue so vividly, yet we do. Blue is amplified from our hallucination."

Buddy thought briefly and asked, "What about the sky? Was that the color of wine?" Blueman shrugged, "In remote regions of Papua New Guinea, there are tribes that not only lack the color blue in their vocabulary, but they recognize it as a shade of green." Buddy asked, "But why Blue?" Blueman speculated, "Why do television stations use a green screen?" Buddy knew this one, "Because that green is a color that's never found in nature." Blueman said, "Exactly. Neither is blue. It's the rarest color in nature." Buddy pointed up, "But the sky is blue." Blueman responded, "We hallucinate the sky to be blue, Buddy. No matter where you point your eyes, there is no way to stare directly at the color blue. It's impossible. That veil could be hiding anything." Buddy asked, "So when I see blue, what am I looking at?" Blueman answered, "Mythology calls it Hades. The underworld is the unseen world." Buddy replied, "So the sky could be a cosmic green screen?" Blueman nodded, "I guess it could." Buddy replied, "I still don't believe you."

Buddy built up his nerve, "I never thought I'd be asking this, but can you tell me about my aura?" Blueman laughed, handed Buddy his glass, and said, "Sure, pour me a drink." Buddy obliged so Blueman could watch his frame as he worked. Blueman delivered the reading, "You love to sail, and it probably came from a fear of flying." Buddy tried to hold his poker face, and Blueman saw through his reaction, "You have feelings for her, and most of your energy is spent covering those tracks." Buddy dropped a cube of ice into the glass and whistled, "Damn." He was completely naked under Blueman's nose, and he felt it. Blueman held him there longer before saying, "I know who it is because you vibrate around her. That doesn't happen with Rose." Buddy was tangibly flustered. Blueman didn't stop, "Right now, you feel intimidated. But, I don't intimidate you, Buddy. I see you. Being seen is what you find so intimidating. This is why a horse wears blinders. They do this to feel less intimidated."

Buddy admitted it, "I've got goosebumps. The hairs on my neck are standing straight up. You can see this? What color is my aura?" Blueman shook his head, "You have to rethink what aura means. You don't see the light; you render its musk. Buddy held up his hands and tried to look at them differently but couldn't. Blueman told him, "It's like believing in electricity. You feel electricity, but you don't see it, correct?" Buddy answered, "Yes." Blueman said, "As the aperture receives light, a limbic aura is built to display its information. This display doesn't have to be visual. You have an entire limbic system to display information. You can hallucinate sound, voice, light, shadow, feelings, sensations, and memories. All of these are auric information. When we digest food, the aura is how food feels. Not just its flavor on our tongue but the way it plays our mood. This is perceivable information encoded in a field we can see if we relax." Buddy asked, "Why do I have to relax?" Blueman answered, "The body can only digest food when it feels safe and comfortable. The eye of consciousness works the same." Buddy said, "Then why use methamphetamine? Isn't that the opposite of relaxing?" Blueman answered, "The aperture is a muscle that must be torn before it can carry any weight."

Blueman asked Buddy, "Consider the consequences of never being able to lie. That naked feeling you felt when I saw your aura would be unacceptable for most people. No one would socialize if they couldn't lie. The world pretends the truth isn't under its nose when it is. Ectohormones occupy the pores of our skin, hovering in the heartbeat's tide. We are haunted by chemical apparitions summoned by ourselves and others." Buddy jested, "Until we have a shower." Blueman agreed, "Or a baptism. Smell is the oldest form of nudity. Long before we cared about how we looked, we cared about our smell. Pheromones are organic circuits. Electronics have diodes, gates, and capacitors. Pheromones have signalers, modulators, and releasers. Our nervous system is hard-wired into the olfactory grid. Chemosignals have full access to the nervous system and can trigger anxiety, relaxation, trust, hunger, and even reproduction."

Buddy asked, "So humans wear horse-blinders to lie to each other?" Blueman answered, "And themselves. Ever notice when something horrible is about to happen, someone insists that everything will be okay?" Buddy nodded, "Famous last words." Blueman replied, "Denial and ignorance are the body's immune response. We couldn't do that if we smelled the whole truth."

Buddy commented, "This is why horses spook so easily; they smell too much." Blueman agreed, "If a stranger is civilized, you are comfortable around them. If they are consistently civilized over time, you may trust them enough to turn your back. How can you be comfortable around something that smells dangerous?" Buddy replied, "You can't." Blueman agreed, "That's right. You have two choices. You can keep your fancy nose detector and abandon civilization or abandon your nose and enjoy the bliss of strangers."

Buddy raised his glass and gave a toast, "To deodorant — the pillar of civilization." Blueman chuckled, "There's a college in New York that collected the armpit sweat from twenty skydivers on their first jump. They put the sweat in a nebulizer and exposed it to a volunteer in a brain scanner. The volunteers' amygdala and hypothalamus activated the same way as the skydivers terrified of jumping. Their fear was fully transmitted through the sweat's chemosignature."

Buddy was impressed, "Wow." Blueman said, "Here's the thing. The volunteer wasn't able to consciously tell you what his nose could. There was no conscious connection between his olfactory. His body knew the fear completely, but the sensation did not reach his neo-cortex. Modern man has severed the cord between him and smell. The smell is the underworld of chemosignals. All of its information is sacrificed for the community."

CHAPTER TEN

Jambazi

Linus was perched on the fire escape underneath the constellations when he saw Blueman for the first time. He heard a question as two men walked below him across the courtyard, "How much do you offer for an albino?" A man in blue made no reply. He was a stoic ghost with a singular purpose. Linus wondered if they were clients of Buddy's in the market for clones.

His answer shrank as it walked away in the night. But even Linus knew better than to approach a human trafficker and ask him about their business. It was then the blue one stopped. His voice commanded Linus as it echoed off the walls in the courtyard, "You there. The man on the balcony who thinks he's invisible. Join us for a drink, why don't you?"

Linus accepted the invitation but was too petrified to say. He collected himself and found the blue man in the pool house. Linus broke the ice, "How did you know I was up there?" The man answered plainly, "I saw you." Linus asked him, "Do you have eyes in the back of your head?" He grabbed an extra glass and answered, "Why yes if we count my occipital lobe. I'm Blueman; pleased to meet you." Linus shook his hand and said in jest, "Of course you are."

Blueman had heard these jokes before, "Your couch treats epilepsy, correct?" Linus nodded, "It stimulates the vagus nerve." Blueman nodded, "But what about an epileptic seizure? Could it stop one of those?" Linus considered his question carefully, "It could, but I don't know how you'd get the patient to sit still long enough for my equipment to find the nerve. The body is seizing after all." Blueman was impressed, "How does a couch find a vagus nerve? "Linus joked, "It has eyes in the back of its head." Blueman smiled. Linus continued, "My couch could prevent a seizure before it happened because it would see it coming in the pulse. But they'd need to be on the couch first, so it has a baseline." Blueman nodded and asked the question he wanted answered, "Could the chair activate a seizure?" Before Linus could answer, a phone rang. Blueman's companion answered the call and listened quietly. He ended the call and told Blueman, "We have a deal."

Blueman had been on a quest to capture albinism in a vial. Unlocking the secrets of melanin had been his Holy Grail. People with albinism are a commodity in Africa for many reasons. For Blueman, it was their ability to see reality. The albino eye sees a world that's unfiltered by melanin. This blessing is a curse that crucifies them in many ways. People with albinism are more likely to suffer from schizophrenia and other mental illnesses, and Blueman believes this is a side effect of overexposure. Tanzania is the epicenter of albinism. You are twenty-five times more likely to find a person with albinism there. The cradle of civilization has always been the fountainhead for new inventions, and the person with albinism is Africa's fruit. There are 150,000 albinos in Tanzania, and everyone is a hunted ghost. They are called "Zeru Zeru," a zero or a nobody.

In Swahili, the root word for insane means to be sincere or transparent. To be crazy, or wazimu, is to carry no lies.

Without melanin, the person with albinism suffers from exposure. He has no way to shade his eyes. In Tanzania, he, like all white-skins, is mzungu. These people are forced to constantly turn themselves in a circle to survive the sun's beating. This makes their soul hollow like an empty walking ghost, and Blueman is about to purchase one.

Giraffes hum before dawn. Their vocal cords are too long to sing. Venus rose in a purple cloak as the men loaded the car. Rose gave Blueman the paperwork and wished them safety through the gauntlet of Machafuko, "Rudi karibuni."

Machafuko is a horrid place. Sawa's cousin had albinism. She lost both of her hands when a man hacked them off with a machete. The mother saw the motorcycle driving away with their pieces. The albino lives in Hell. They are the rejects of the rejected. Sawa's eyes were five years old when Jambazi called them his trophy. The man launched his decree at the market, standing from the cockpit of his jeep. He told the mother, "Those eyes are mine, sister. I will pluck them when they are ripe." Sawa did not blink as he burned a hole through the gangster. Jambazi didn't like feeling naked, so he pulled a handgun from his chest and fired into the air for attention, "Zeru's eyes are mine. Macho ni Yangu!" Sawa's mother ran them both into the sanctuary of the market.

Jambazi was a powerful cheetah, and the people respected his property. As instructed, no one bothered Sawa. In a few years, his home became a shrine. People would leave gifts with prayers attached and even money. Sawa's health became a symbol of Jambazi's dominance. Before the sun was up, Sawa awoke to his mother rushing outside into the street, pleading, "Wait. Wait." The street was quiet except for the idling motor of a moped. Sawa saw his mother clutching the driver's arm, begging him to tell her, "Who sent you? Who?" The driver freed his arm and drove away, saying nothing. Sawa's mom shouted blessings, "Mungu akubariki!"

Sawa was twelve when Jambazi's man pulled outside his home and started honking, "Zeru Zeru, where are you? Jambazi wants to see you." Sawa approached the moped and told the driver he was busy. "You are busy, Sawa? Really? Do you know what a bounce in the ass it is to get up this hill? Don't be a Zuzu. Get on before we are both grumpy." Sawa relented and climbed on before it caused a scene. Sawa's mother came out as they drove away, saying, "Where are you going?" Sawa waved a kiss and reassured her, "Kurudi Karibuni."

Jambazi's empire had thrived in seven years, and his demeanor and territory had matured. Sawa was brought to his house overlooking a hill of fruit trees and seated on the couch to wait. Jambazi finished a phone call and sat down in front of Sawa. He said, "Do you remember what I told you about your eyes, Sawa?" Sawa answered, "You called them nyara." Jambazi was pleased and asked, "Do you think your mother remembers?" Sawa looked into his lap, ashamed. Jambazi continued, "I respect your burden. I am not your enemy. Help me with my trophy. I can make it so your mom will never know. You and I can do business as men, and she can live a life of peace." Jambazi gave Sawa some time to think, but it didn't help. He said, "Time is up, Sawa. What is your decision?"

Emotional tears appear to be unique to Homo Sapiens. Tears are the exit of salt and potassium, both carriers of experience. If the spine were a cobra, the Periaqueductal Gray would be its throat. This place is called the PAG, the throat of emotion. You'd pinch this spot if you wanted to see man's fangs. Tears are the PAG lubricating itself under heavy emotional bandwidth. We cry when we are excessively happy or sad. We cry when we are overly inspired or moved. Sawa had no tears. Sawa had already mourned his loss. Sawa had been having nightmares about this day, and here it was. He said, "How do I give them to you?" Jambazi handed Sawa a business card and said, "See this man. He will tell your mother your eyes have cancer." Four months later, Sawa was prepped for surgery.

His mother's scent was enough to bring him out of anesthesia. He could tell she was sad, but his memory was clouded as to why. The precious moments of ignorance were evaporating quickly. Sawa would remember he gave his eyes so his mother would not see the truth. His fingers crawled their way up his face and felt the dressing. An unknown hand grabbed his arm and placed it back on the bed, saying, "Acha." Plastic shells filled his eye sockets. Holes for ventilation had been cut where his pupils used to rest, but he could not see. Sawa slowly remembered what had happened. He heard his mother sobbing through his bandages. The doctor was giving her instructions like she was learning a new appliance. He told her, "Tomorrow, we can remove the dressing. The socket will look red but turn pink as it heals. I'd like you to meet Dr Blueman."

Sawa's mother explained her apprehensions about Sawa leaving his village to the doctor. She insisted Sawa would be happier here where the blessings have flowed. Blueman assured her by saying, "I know you'll do what's best for Sawa." Blueman was the first person Sawa met without his sight. He could feel the man's pulse telegraphing through each sentence. Sawa had never bothered to see a voice before. His vision was always too busy painting pictures.

The surgeon spoke plainly to Sawa's mom, "After this, do you think your village will still consider Sawa good luck? You know what happens. His arms and limbs will be next. This man can help, but Sawa must go with him." Blueman handed Sawa's mother a folder and said, "This is the contract." The surgeon implored her to sign, "Jambazi already has his fruit. He has lost the motivation to protect you."

That night, Sawa could not sleep. He felt bursts of energy hitting the back of his eye. He could not shut off the lights that kept pulsing. Spitting hammers made their way to the back of his brain as if he were plugged into a wall socket. Outside his blindness, the room was dark. Pulses of light were coming from underneath Sawa's gauze. A tiny microcontroller had been wired to his optic nerve, keeping it alive. The pulses he saw were the system constantly stimulating the neural pathways. Dr Blueman believed this was the only way to keep the nerves alive.

Blueman came to make his rounds, and Sawa asked if they were alone. Dr Blueman closed the door, sat beside Sawa, and said, "Yes. We are alone." Sawa cupped his hand over his right eye and said, "This eye does not hurt. How come?" Blueman joked, "Are you complaining?" Sawa said," No." Blueman replied, "Jambazi only needed one to prove his point." Sawa asked, "Did Jambazi tell you this?" Blueman responded, "No. This is what I told Jambazi." Sawa almost said thank you, but Blueman stopped him. He assured Sawa, "Only in Hell would a boy who lost his eye say thank you. You will remain blind for some time, Sawa. The implant needs to be the only input until the pathways form." Sawa asked, "How long until I can see again?" Blueman said, "That's between you and your stem cells. Somewhere between six months and never. How's that for an answer?" Sawa was still coming out ahead from where he was this morning.

Blueman adjusted Sawa's microcontroller so he could sleep. Dr. Blueman said, "Do you understand what Jambazi would do if people found out you still had an eye?" Sawa replied, "He would take the other one." Blueman agreed, "Worse. Only you can decide if your mom should know. Until then, the dressings will keep your secret." Sawa could see nothing through his dressings, yet he felt Blueman leave the room. His body was an electrical antenna, and it sensed the room change. Sawa would not have felt this experience before the blindness. An entire world has appeared from his loss of sight.

CHAPTER ELEVEN

Implant

Melanin is a human chlorophyll that converts sunlight into human energy. Melanin is a black hole where no light escapes. Melanin absorbs X-ray and ultraviolet light, storing it indefinitely. It erases photons as if they were never there. It absorbs the energy of anything that tries to touch it. It swallows reality with its relentless appetite.

There are five types of melanin in the body. It does so much more than color our skin. We find it in the nasal cavity. We find it inside the darkest parts of the inner ear where no sunlight can reach. We find it in the deepest parts of our brainstem and spine. Its molecular characteristics are so fundamental that melanin's chemical composition hasn't changed in 150 million years. Melanin from the Jurassic era found inside the fossilized sack of ancient squid is still capable of photovoltaic conductivity.

Sawa has no melanin. When Sawa had eyes, they would quiver in their sockets. This is the norm, not the exception, with albinism. The shaking decreases with age and will usually stop by seven. Albinism always accompanies poor eyesight. The body reacts to an unfiltered world by trying to dilute the screen. The jitters are a protest to its permanence.

Albinism is a constant war with duality. Lacking binocular vision, the albino sees from both eyes but can't see the same object with both eyes simultaneously. All of this comes from the lack of melanin.

Linus found Blueman in the lab with Sawa and said, "Buddy said you could use some help?" Blueman was perturbed, "I asked for Buddy. Where is he?" Linus explained, "Tack room. Something about Leda. He asked if I was around, so here I am." Blueman expected Linus to say no when he asked, "Do you know how to hook up a patient monitor?" Linus looked around, pointed at the monitor in the corner, and asked, "That one?" Blueman nodded and told him to get busy. The moment Sawa sat in the exam chair, he felt uncomfortable. Linus noted the rise in pulse immediately. Blueman was calibrating Sawa's pupil monitor and ordered Sawa to relax, which had the opposite effect. Linus encouraged Sawa with an exaggerated gulp, "Swallow with me, Sawa. Like this." Blueman said, "I'm going to give Sawa a local anesthetic. I need you to watch these vitals." Blueman pointed to the monitor. Linus agreed, wanting to impress Blueman.

Surgery wasn't Blueman's strong suit, but he was more than qualified. Attaching the neural moss to Sawa's retinal wall took him less than an hour. The implant was farmed like a rice patty from the outer layer of a donor cortex, but Linus didn't ask where he got it. It squished its way into the cavern of Sawa's eye and made itself a home. Linus seemed interested, so Blueman explained, "Sawa already knows he can't believe his eyes. The rest of us are still walking around in the dark. The eyes are here to paint a commission of what's possible. Hades is the rest of the world underneath. These two places exist in stereo. One is seen. One is unseen. Sawa's injury gives us a rare opportunity to capture and compare the difference."

Linus asked, "Hades? Wow. That sounds pretty dark." Blueman corrected him, "Hades isn't dark. Hades is hidden. It's easy to conflate the two, but they are very different. Sawa sees both. He has done this since birth. This is why his eyes would quiver. The mind jumps back and forth between what is seen and what is hidden."

Linus asked, "So Hades is here; we just can't see it?" Blueman confirmed with a grunt as he began the final incision. After a few minutes, he continued, "You know how the astronomers declared Pluto was no longer a planet?" Linus answered, "Yeah, that was kinda dumb." Blueman finished, "It's like Pluto. Pluto is still there. We stopped admitting it. That's Hades. Everything we ignore is cast into Hades." Linus speculated, "So Hades is where we deny things exist?" Blueman agreed, clarifying, "Hades is where we deny things out of existence. Ignoring something doesn't make it go away — it makes it invisible. See the difference?"

Linus thought for a minute and tested his understanding, "So Sawa sees both worlds simultaneously?" Blueman responded, "It's worse because his reality can't decide which world to believe, so it constantly flickers between them. Albinos are not alone. Pretty much anyone with crossed eyes or strabismus suffers from the same thing. Poor eyesight could be understood so much better as an immune response. The same response is a factor in schizophrenic hallucinations and psychotropic visions. The mind is splintered between two scenes as it stares directly into the burning sun." Linus noticed, "Sounds like Hell." Blueman agreed, "Helios is made of helium. That's Hell on earth for the person with albinism."

Linus asked Blueman, "How does this neural moss help Sawa see?" Blueman said, "It doesn't. It records what his thalamus chose to ignore. Sawa already perceives Hades. All of us do. The neural moss will capture signals coming into Sawa's eye from his brain." Linus was confused, "So Hades is inside his brain?" Blueman said, "The raw feed of what Hades looks like is inside. We can determine what the mind chooses to ignore by tracking the efferent neurons in the retinal pipe. Eyes aren't like cameras. Eyes are more like cave paintings." Blueman adjusted his magnifier and pointed to the screen, "These nerves are coming into the eye from the brain. The mind will tell the epithelial body which receptors are sensing too much pain and secrete melanin to absorb that limbic voltage." Linus was intrigued, "Like tiny shutters?" Blueman marveled, "Yes. This is the role of melanin. It swallows the eye's vision directly at the cone. Every rod and cone is controlled by dopamine and melanin. This is how we feel the beauty in a sunset or the terror in a fire. This shock is communicated to and from the eyes, and the parts that are too painful can be dimmed accordingly." Linus was excited, "So one has to be comfortable to see Hades?" Blueman nodded, "It's the only way." Linus continued, "So if I could relax enough, I would see ghosts?" Blueman nodded, "Yes, if you mean ghost, as in the plasma that haunts someone." Linus said, "Really? But how?" Blueman said, "When people lie, the nose knows. It sensates their pheromones and renders them on your screen. When the aperture is open, you see people in their entirety, and let me tell you, banshees are terrifying."

Linus asked, "What's the difference between a ghost and a banshee?" Blueman answered him, "Banshees are the polar opposite of ghosts. Ghosts are possessed plasma charged with a desire to complete something. A banshee is made to reject or break something. The olfactory show you these things." Linus' face was stunned, "And you see them? Like floating around." Blueman said, "I animize them into my hallucination. You do this on a fundamental level, but your brain labels it as spam because it's overwhelmingly unpleasant to experience. But trust me. Your intuition knows.

Every pheromone moving through the aether can be sensed and felt in the underworld."

Linus asked, "But what exactly do you and Sawa see that I don't? What does Hades look like?" Blueman laughed, "You still don't understand the eyes. Hades is felt, not seen. In Hades, you understand more because you witness its scent. Everything kind of pulses in Hades. Each surge unfolds a deeper flavor the more you remain in its taste. You behold Hades more than you see it. It possesses you because that's what pheromones are — possessions."

Linus asked Blueman, "How did you discover this place?" Blueman replied, "I got sad enough to stop closing my eyes. The more pain I saw, the deeper I went. I found the darkest blues I've ever seen and went deeper. Hades is a willingness to pour compassion into the darkness, and darkness is never shallow. It's a pilgrimage into the abyss, searching for everything you rejected. Once you know Hades is there, you learn to sense it even deeper. Sawa is here to teach me how far it goes." Linus retorted, "If you can't see without practice, how do you know you're not hallucinating?" Blueman answered unapologetically, "You don't."

Linus said again, "What I mean is, maybe Sawa can't see depth because depth isn't real?" Blueman concurred, "That wouldn't surprise me. We live in Sarabi, the world of illusion, or Maya. Ever think about why Krishna and Vishnu are blue?" Linus answered, "Wasn't Krishna poisoned at birth?" Blueman was impressed, "Indeed he was. The reality of the world was so toxic his skin turned blue. And Krishna wasn't the only blue lord. Rama, Vishnu, Kali, and Shiva were also blue. The Egyptian gods Amun and Amon were blue, too. Amon's name means the hidden one. Our mythology tells us the Lord of Hades is blue, again, the link between blue and the unseen. Sawa's eyes are blue, as are most people affected by albinism."

Linus replied, "The sky is blue." Blueman replied, "Sort of. The sky is more gray than blue. We chose the molecules we deemed important and amplified them in our viewport. We do the same with flowers. Our cave painting makes the sky blue. We live in a hyper-reality of hallucinated information transposed by what's important for our survival. We don't see. We commission a hallucination and show that to ourselves for tactical purposes."

Several minutes passed, and Blueman noticed the time, "You know why sloths move so slowly? They are blind in the daylight. Their eyes decided a long time ago color wasn't important. These creatures live longer than we do, and they abandon their cones entirely. They don't need them." Linus considered as he watched Sawa's vitals, "This must be how dogs see smells, huh?" Blueman said, "Maybe. You'll have to ask Buddy about that one. He's the vet." Blueman carefully submerged and removed a gold transistor board with tiny titanium hairs from a flask of melanin. Blueman said, "See those tiny hairs? There are over a million of them. This implant will give us a resolution of 1024x1024 at the fovea." Blueman inserted the chip into the newly installed bed of neural moss and saturated the area with melanin from an eye dropper, sealing it up like a crankcase. Linus was wincing sympathetically for Sawa as he imagined a million fishhooks sinking into the back of his eyes. Finally, Blueman inflated a tiny balloon inside the mold and told Sawa, "Hard part's over. You're basically home. Lay still till the cement cures."

Blueman rolled across the room and began to write something in a chart. Linus followed him, almost whispering, "I wanna see Hades." Blueman was too busy recording some notes. Linus asked again, "Can I be a test subject?" Blueman ignored him. Linus assured him, "I'd sign a waiver or whatever?" Linus didn't realize how loud he had gotten when he said, "Blueman. I wanna see!" Blueman stopped abruptly and looked up, "That's what everyone says till they do."

For five moons, Sawa enjoyed the benefits of blindness. He noticed how calm he felt in its water. He wasn't sure if he'd ever see another face, but it almost didn't matter. Every stranger he ever met would usually give him an expression of shock or horror. His future was bright in the darkness. Blueman taught Sawa echolocation with a pair of spoons from Rose's kitchen. He clicked out a tour for Sawa through the dining room, explaining, "All you need is sound." Blueman urged Sawa, "It will feel impossible because the mind is still lying. Don't believe it. You have to guess, Sawa! Guess, again and again, over and over. Keep convincing yourself the guessing works because it does."

For weeks, Linus helped Sawa practice, and Sawa improved. One day, Sawa felt the moon rise. He dragged Rose out of the stable and pointed into the sky, "Miss Vega, tell me please, is the moon right there?" Rose was astounded. She wanted Blueman to explain how two spoons could track where the moon was in the daytime. Blueman told her, "The spoons were a crutch Sawa needed to tap into his blindsight." Rose asked, "Blindsight?" Blueman nodded, "The eyes don't need a visual cortex to see. Blindsight has been proven to exist in the brains of monkeys. The human brain is stubborn, though. It has grown accustomed to sight and has trouble tapping into its underlying intuition. By encouraging Sawa to believe, he is tapping into his other senses and building a model he can visualize without his eyes."

CHAPTER TWELVE

Bident

Months passed, and Linus became obsessed with Blueman's work. In particular with Leda's epilepsy. He decided to upgrade Rose's therapy chair with a new headpiece. The innards were splayed out on the table when Linus asked Sawa for assistance, "I need the yellow screwdriver." Sawa bobbed his head from side to side, sounding the toolbox. He could hear three screwdrivers, but color wasn't something he detected. Sawa sensed the density of each handle, but that didn't help. He decided yellow was rubbery, so he grabbed it, hoping for the best.

Two electrified tuning forks had been wired into a guitar amplifier on the workbench. Linus tweaked the potentiometers on each until they shared a common frequency. The table shook when they found their harmony. Once tuned, he slid the forks into a carbon fiber sleeve and announced his invention, "I present the sonoluminescent trident!" Linus reflected momentarily, realizing his trident only had two prongs, "Correction. The sonoluminescent bident!" The bident stimulated any part of the body by creating an acoustic bubble out of two sounds. Linus told Sawa, "It's like smacking your hands together underwater really fast." This made sense to Sawa. The bident was secured to a circular gantry and mounted to the chair.

Linus lacked the esteem to fail in the eyes of anyone but Sawa. Linus told him, "When I say ready. Push this switch. Got it?" Sawa nodded, "No problem." Linus said again, "No matter what happens, turn it off after you count to three." Sawa nodded, "No problem." Linus repeated, "No matter what my face does. Turn it off." Sawa nodded again, "I understand." Linus considered his life choices and still went ahead and placed his head inside the gantry. He strapped his chin into the dome and handed his brain to a blind teenager and a toggle switch. Linus took one last breath and braced himself as he commanded Sawa, "Hit me!"

Sawa pushed the button, and Linus heard Sawa laugh maniacally. At least Linus thought it was Sawa. But Sawa's face was not moving. Linus thought this was funny, so he laughed. At least, this is how his brain reasoned what had happened. For the count of three, Linus held no volition and could not accept that he was the only one laughing. The bident stimulated his brain while his mind reverse engineered an explanation. After counting three, Sawa turned the switch off, returning Linus' brain to its owner. Linus noticed Sawa looked horrified at what he had just done. Linus' brain laughed again, but for real this time, and Linus assured Sawa, " It's okay, Sawa. It works!"

Linus unhooked himself from the chair and contemplated its implications. Not only could he manipulate the spine and the vagus, but he could directly massage the brain electromagnetically. Linus was elated and showcased his upgrade to Blueman. When Blueman finally came to see, Linus said, "I was inspired by your work." Blueman seemed unimpressed and teased him, saying, "It looks like one of those dryers you see at a hair salon."

Later that moon, Sawa's stem cells finally grew enough to

cut through the neural moss and strike light. The dam broke under a geyser of photons pouring down Sawa's optic river. His head throbbed from the gushing flow of potassium. It felt like a bayonet stabbing the root of his eye, but Sawa kept looking as instructed. It got better after he noticed the pain surging with the rhythm of his heart. It wasn't pain at all. It was the flow of new information. Blueman told Sawa all pain is information and perception has a price. Sawa could not believe the joy he felt from so much discomfort. A few days later, Blueman removed the hermetic seal from Sawa's eye, restoring his vision. As Dr. Blueman had hoped, Sawa had full vision from his left eye and a working implant in his right.

Lyra came ripping through the house like a jet fight into the kitchen, panting, "Rose! Rose! It's Sawa." Lyra took a breath, "He's riding the bicycle. Quick!" Rose wiped her hands and rushed outside. As Lyra promised, Sawa rode a yellow bicycle in a circle with a big smile. Rose covered her mouth to hide the inadequacy of words as Lyra joined him in a parade around the driveway. Rose uncovered her mouth long enough to tell Lyra, "Slow down." Sawa laughed as he replied, "I see her, Miss Vega. I see you, too. I see everything!"

CHAPTER THIRTEEN

Rose

It was happy hour, and Rose took her boots off and placed them under the bench to go inside. She preferred her sessions with Linus in the afternoon. It gave her a chance to work and feed the stock. Blueman saw his opportunity and pounced on Rose, "We need a sperm sample from Sawa. Can you talk to him?" Rose asked why, but Blueman was vague, "A couple of reasons." Rose waited before asking, "Well? Are you going to give me one?" Blueman relented, "I think his sperm might have what it takes to save the egg harvest." Rose peered into him like a closed storefront, "Sawa isn't museum stock." Blueman disagreed, "Sawa signed a contract just like Leda. Leda gave us eggs. Sawa can give us sperm. I thought he'd take it better from you, is all. Should I have Buddy tell him?"

Rose grumbled up the stairs, landed on Linus' couch, and said, "Hit me." Linus could see Rose was near tears, "Wow. I see we have some work to do. Let's start with that neck, shall we?" The chair began to hum, and Rose sank deeper in every tone. Her breathing changed its rhythm as she found a better gear. Linus monitored her progress, "Now we're cruising. How do you feel?" Rose didn't talk but realized she wasn't mad at Blueman. She was angry at God for giving her a barren stable surrounded by all this fertility. She felt mocked in her family business, her attempts at conception, this human egg farm, and now everyone's obsession with Leda. Rose felt dry and crumbled on a continent where everything was blooming. Linus noticed her pulse soothe as he modulated a new sweep. Rose relaxed and said, "Wherever you are doing, don't stop."

Rose drifted back to their farm in Virginia. She was spraying down Powhatan, her painted mare. Buddy could be heard orating the opportunities of Africa from the barn, but she wasn't listening. The water's prism shattered the sunlight into a rainbow that Powhatan was watching. Rose asked her for confirmation, which she gave telepathically. Horses are known to twitch an ear when ending their transmission. Buddy repeated himself because Rose wasn't listening, "There are gene therapies available outside the country." Buddy came out of the barn, but Powhatan stomped and snorted her disapproval. Rose scolded, "Buddy! Get out of here. How can you be so thick." Buddy felt shame from Rose's rebuke and hustled back inside, embarrassed. Yesterday morning, Buddy shot both of Powhatan's foals shortly after they were born. The American Painted Horse is marked for death in its genes. A genetic disorder similar to albinism haunts its offspring. Blue-eyed foals are born solid white and lack a functioning colon. They die a horrible death if no one is there to put them out of their misery. Rose had a good cry over Powhatan. It was the closest she could get to mourning what was bothering her.

If misery were wings, all of us could fly. But heaven holds no tolerance. Heaven banishes suffering to the underworld, where no one has to see if they don't want to. Hades is the only place for misery to go because it's the only place it can be itself in peace. Linus continued to modulate Rose through the dials on his chair. He dipped her like a dolphin through the surf. The body doesn't thrive in stillness. It wants story, rhythm, and pulse. Every scalar wave has three expressions, and knowing how to use them is the secret to Linus' music.

Linus forgot his place and asked, "Why does Blueman always wear blue? He doesn't just wear it; he lives it?" Rose half-answered from the bottom of the chair, "He said it makes him invisible." Linus chuckled from behind her and said, "Of course he did. Invisible. I should have known." The laugh taunted Rose to insist playfully, "Tell him, Blueman." Linus jolted as he looked up, expecting Blueman in the room. Rose giggled at his gullibility and said, "Got you. But you know something? It works." Linus wasn't sure if Rose was still pulling his leg, "Fool me twice, Rose?" Rose swore from the altar of her chest, "No. There is a farm in Australia. Blueman has livestock there who can't see him. All of the staff wear blue. The observation buildings are painted blue — every piece. Every screw is blue. Every tile. Every door knob. Every window. Even the golf cart is blue. Even its wheels." Linus' eyes were bulging at the seams, "But why?" Rose answered him with a shrug, "Camouflage. Enrichment. Landscape immersion. He insists it works." Linus was shocked, "That's impossible. Even if that were true, blue would just appear gray. Right?" Rose replied, "He said blue is a forbidden color. Something about the brain cancels it out when its complement is displayed. Certain colors in the primitive brain will disappear or appear during a fear response because of it." Linus proposed, "Like seeing red?" Rose replied, "Or green with envy." Linus asked, "So color-blind people can't see Blueman?" Rose answered, "Color blind people with a 100,000-year-old brain can't see Blueman because the future is too scary." Linus was floored, "But his shadow, his smell, his breathing? That can't be possible." Rose replied, "Blueman says it works because their mind decides it is too expensive to render, so they dismiss the data." Linus asked, "How did

Blueman find a 100,000-year-old aborigine?" Rose chuckled, "He didn't. As I said, the museum keeps a living collection. The charter runs everything. The museum. Shamba Macho. The jet that brought you here. The camp in Australia. Just like Buddy, Blueman has a contract to deliver something." Linus asked, "Deliver what?" Rose shrugged, "Eye serum, maybe? He's pretty hush about it. But why are we talking during my happy hour?" Linus corrected his breach and got back to his music.

CHAPTER FOURTEEN

Dubai

Blueman was one of the few contractors who reported directly to the museum board. It's why he spent so much time away from the shamba. When Blueman told them how long it took him to drive to the nearest airport, he thought they would leave him to work peacefully. Instead, they commissioned the nearest village to develop a private runway. The gesture gave Blueman no excuse to rest easy, and the private jet raised the stakes on everything expected from him.

Blueman had already proven his utility to the museum. A lightweight consumer version of his serum was in market testing as high-definition eyedrops. The therapy amplifies the retina's photoreceptive proteins, allowing the brain to see in higher resolution. The literature featured an ophthalmologist pointing at an eye chart with a solid pink square, asking the patient if he could "See Seven Colors?" With the eyedrops, the pink square revealed seven degrees of color between pink and purple. Each square was labeled: Pirk, Punkle, Pinple, Punk, Purk, Punple, and Purkle.

The museum asked Blueman to bring Leda to Dubai for a meeting. Blueman made her swear she wouldn't sign anything without showing him first. Blueman did his best to explain to Leda the customs of Dubai, but she kept laughing at how silly it sounded, "You have a jet that can go anywhere, and you take me to a place where it's wrong to kiss in public?" Blueman ignored the question and asked Leda, "Why are you wearing war paint?" Leda laughed as she touched her neck, "Did you just call my eye shadow warpaint? Blueman replied, "Isn't eye shadow supposed to go on the eyes? You look like a blue panda." Leda said, "Thank you. I thought it would be sweet if we matched. But if you don't like it, mister blue man, you can take it off and decorate me however you like." Blueman exhaled as he looked out the window at Kilimanjaro. Leda told him, "Faith brought us here. Look how high we are together. How many people in the world are as fortunate as us? Not many, I bet." Leda was sitting on Blueman's lap. Blueman scolded Leda with his eyes and said, "You can't do this in Dubai." Leda got closer, "I guess we'll have to do it here then." Blueman scolded her more, "If they arrest you, I won't be able to stop them." Leda laughed, "Not true. You would find a way to stop them." Blueman couldn't help but smile. He drank Leda through his nose, knowing it won't be long before she would share her feelings with the cockpit.

They landed in Dubai, where a vehicle took them into the city. A silver airship was docked high above them as they entered the ground floor of the building's towering spire. Blueman's stomach dropped as the magnetic elevator shot them one hundred stories into the air without a sound. He waited patiently inside a quiet, menacing lobby. He could not sit as his spine was transmitting too much electricity. The people inside were influential, and Blueman could feel them in his bones. They understood the crucible of time and demanded gold from each moment. Up here, the air is thin. Every molecule matters if you want to keep breathing.

The board room doors opened like a city gate, and Blueman entered. A large round table filled with spectators surrounded him. He finished his presentation by saying, "Unpacking a species like that requires multiple generations, not one. As the saying goes, you will need two of every kind."

A man in green asked, "I'm new here, but why two? Can't we clone a sheep from a single mammary cell?" Blueman answered, "Visit the Australian habitat, and you'll see why. The population is clumsy and unable to run or hunt. They are barely able to gather food left by the warden." The man asked, "How do you know two generations is enough?" Blueman answered, "Consider the success of Homo Erectus, Homo Heidelbergensis, and Homo Sapiens Sapiens. All three are from an otherwise extinct genus. Lightning will strike the same place twice if the conditions are right." The green man asked, "How long does the seed need to sprout?" Blueman guessed, "I'd say at least fifteen hundred years." The man balked at the timeline, "That's a long time." Blueman retorted, "I disagree. Two hundred thousand years is a long time. What I am suggesting is a shortcut."

The man in white's name was Solomon, and Blueman knew him well. Solomon asked, "What happened with the eggs, Dr. Blueman?" Blueman tried to dodge, "I addressed that in my report." A woman in violet said she wanted to know more. Blueman flattened his wrinkles and said, "As the report mentions, we have a fertilization issue we are currently solving." Mr. Solomon asked, "How many fertilized eggs are there?" Blueman swallowed, "There is one. But legally, that egg is not under contract." Solomon corrected him, "So the answer is none?" Blueman agreed with the math. The woman asked, "When will the fertilized egg be under contract?" Blueman hesitated, "Eight years to contract. Ten years to harvest." The woman was disappointed, "That's quite a delay." Blueman remained grounded, "The good news here is our candidate is viable for fertilization. As you can see, the eggs are healthy-" Solomon interrupted, "Yes, Dr. Blueman. You mentioned that in your report."

Seventy-two floors below, Leda was in a conference room selling her body to the museum. Page four awarded her ten million dollars if she delivered a baby. The lawyer asked, "Do you have any questions about page six?" Leda looked at her funny and said, "Should I?" The lawyer replied, "Do you understand what paragraph six means? If a physician determines the baby is critical, they can terminate your life prematurely to preserve their property." Leda didn't budge as she said, "And?" The lawyer explained, "This would revoke your right to preservation." Leda said squarely, "I have other rights."

The lawyer explained the confirmation procedure and asked Leda, "Do you have any questions before you confirm?" Leda said, "Where's the money?" The lawyer returned to page four and explained the payment schedule again, but Leda stopped her, "You don't understand. I need the down payment now. In a suitcase. Something to match my eyes, maybe?" The lawyer was dismissive, "We don't have a million dollars in a suitcase." Leda relaxed and said, "That's okay. I'll wait." The lawyer attempted to deliberate, so Leda struck again, "I'll add one more condition since you are still here. In exchange for my right to preservation, I want a corporate jet, like you gave Blueman." The lawyer scooped up her paperwork and rose from her chair. She looked at Leda candidly and said, "If I make this happen for you, and you don't confirm, this will humiliate me." Leda said nothing.

A heavy glass wall separated Leda from the main office as she waited in the conference room by herself. She moved to the head of the table and wrapped her thigh over the armrest.

People stared from cubicles at the lion in the zoo. Leda was an emotional pyromaniac, and the people she set ablaze were the only way she could tolerate boredom.

Fifty-three minutes later, the lawyer returned to the conference room and told the four men inside to return to their desks. A white suitcase carried by a security guard was placed on the table and opened for inspection. The lawyer handed Leda a sealed plastic bag with a biohazard emblem. Leda opened it and placed her finger inside a red plastic tube. She squeezed the trigger, releasing a spring-loaded needle into the fleshy pad of her index finger, and pressed it into the blood scanner. Leda stated her name and date of birth for the record. The lawyer read the entire agreement aloud as Leda stared into the camera. She verbally agreed to each term along the way. The whole contract took eighteen minutes to install, upload, and confirm.

The museum recognizes all limbic contracts as valid if they leave an impression inside the cell's RNA. There are seventy-five million sentences in your chromosomes. Bleeding from the skin triggers an immunity response that writes a marker in this record. This marker can be subpoenaed by a court of law and enforced as a binding contract.

Leda waited for Blueman in the sky bar. The pitched glass roof showcased the silver nose of the zeppelin as it kissed the building. Dubai was the capital of wealth, and Leda was its newest millionaire. She ruined it by ordering a drink from the bartender, "I'll have something blue, please, to match my eyes." The bartender obliged and brought Leda a dirty martini in a blue glass with two white olives. A gentleman in a floral shirt and clean trousers asked if he could pay for it and said, "I'm Dennis, the dentist. But that's just a coincidence. I don't play tennis, if that's what you're wondering." Leda introduced herself. Dennis asked her, "Have you been up?" Dennis was pointing at the zeppelin?

Leda answered, "No. Have you?" Dennis replied, "Yep. I'm the ship's dentist." Leda almost spit out her drink. Dennis asked, "What's so funny?" Leda splayed her fingers in apology, "Nothing. It just seems like such a funny job to have on an airship. Right?" Dennis replied, "Many medical procedures are only legal over international waters. Stem cells. Gene therapies. Even gene contracts. I do implants mostly. You can find just about anything on the Pegasus. Even a dentist." Leda's eyes grew as she asked, "Is there a casino?" Dennis replied, "Of course! Would you like to see it?" Leda beamed and said, "Yes!" Dennis said, "You have a great smile. I should know being a dentist." Leda's mood spoiled a bit when she saw Dennis' aura. Like Blueman, this was one of those times she regretted seeing Hades. Dennis had used this line before, and bad things happened. She could smell it on him. A new voice emerged from Leda's left flank, "Hey, pretty lady, this guy isn't giving you any trouble, is he?" Dennis and his friend greeted each other. Dennis pointed at him and said, "Now, this is the guy you want to know onboard the airship." Leda saw Blueman coming out of the elevator. She asked Dennis' friend, "Let me guess. You're the ship's gynecologist?" It was Dennis who almost spit out his drink.

Blueman waited at the perimeter, but Leda never came. She was anchored between her men and wanted Blueman to fetch her. He approached her party and asked, "Shall we go?" Dennis asked Leda, "Who's this? Your Dad?" Leda said nothing. Dennis struggled to look Blueman in the eye, but he couldn't. Blueman asked Leda again, "Shall we?" Leda scolded Blueman, "No. I want to see the flying casino." Leda looked at Dennis and asked, "Can my dad come?"

Blueman wanted to leave but couldn't. He was stuck, and Leda knew it. Did he tell the museum he left her in Dubai? Does he physically drag her into the elevator, or can he walk her through the casino for a while? Leda asked the bartender for her suitcase, which he placed on the counter, reporting, "Wow, this thing is heavy." Leda agreed and opened the suitcase, revealing one million dollars in cash. Blueman was floored and tried to cover the sight with his arms and torso. Leda swatted him to give her space, removed two hundred-dollar bills, and gave them to the bartender, saying, "Thanks for the olives." Leda closed the suitcase and slid it over to Blueman. He was flabbergasted, "I don't know where you got this, but don't give it to me." Leda replied, "But it's too heavy to carry, Daddy."

CHAPTER FIFTEEN

Pegasus

Leda's entourage crossed a hovering gangplank that took them aboard The Silver Pegasus. Its courtyard casino was flanked by two long rows of shops terracing their way up to a water-crystal ceiling. Dennis told Leda it takes several seconds for sunlight to bounce its way through the intricate maze of crystals. It gave the courtyard a dreamy feeling. Leda drank in the view as she circled to capture it all. Dennis asked, "What do you wanna do first?" Blueman began to complain, "Carrying this suitcase is hardly enjoyable. We should take this back to the plane where it's secure."

Leda grabbed the suitcase from Blueman and lugged it over to the roulette table. She told the dealer, "Everything on black, please." Dennis started whooping, "Now we're flying!" Blueman grabbed Leda's arm like a pincer, "What are you doing? This is nuts." Leda told the dealer, "Wait." She opened the suitcase, pulled out a stack of hundreds, and put it in Blueman's breast pocket, "Here. Now It's less crazy." She closed the case and told the dealer again, "All of it on Black, please." Blueman's blood boiled as she listened to Dennis cheer her on. Blueman snapped at him, "Knock it off, would ya? Let her think for a minute." Leda had no reservations, and the pit boss approved the wager. The dealer asked for final bets. Blueman threw down the stack of bills Leda gave him, saying, "All of it on Red, please."

Roulette is the Devil's Wheel because every number from zero to thirty-six stretched around its circumference adds up to 666. The dealer dropped the ivory ball into the centrifuge. It careened its way through a series of staggering jolts, slowly devolving into a wandering hop. Time tolerated its tantrum until it finally abandoned itself into the crevice of Black-33. Leda was a winner. She told Blueman, "That's what you get for betting against me." Blueman wasn't moved, "Is this supposed to impress me?" Dennis was impressed and said, "I am impressed."

Leda grew bitter underneath her grin and told the dealer, "All on Black, please." Neither Blueman nor Leda watched the next ball tacking around the zodiac. It was Dennis who hooted to everyone that Leda won again. A crowd had formed, but Leda and Blueman didn't care. They were staring each other down like cats in the alley. Leda told the dealer again, "Black, please." The dealer spun the wheel as Blueman implored her, "Stop this, please. Take the money and go. Anywhere. Get as far away from me as you need." Dennis was having an orgasm, "You won again?! This is insane!" Leda told the dealer, "Black, please."

Leda had the whole world on her finger. She tried to share it with him but refused. He told her, "Give the money back to the museum. Walk away from everything that's happened." Blueman asked her, "What did you sign, Leda?" The crystal roof exploded with a light show celebrating the big winner on the floor. Dennis was hopping up and down like a game show contestant as Leda told Blueman, "I promised them a baby." Blueman parked on the bluff of what he just heard. Through tears, over the cheering crowd, Leda yelled at the dealer, "Black, please."

Three hours ago, Leda had one million dollars. When the ball stopped on red, she lost sixteen. The Silver Pegasus doesn't broadcast the biggest loser from the ceiling. That information is only viewable in Hades.

Regardless of how you lose, winners are treated big at The Silver Pegasus. Leda opened the envelope given to her by the pit boss and read it aloud to her companions, "The Captain has invited you to dine with him at his table tonight at seven o'clock." Blueman lost faith in getting out anytime soon. This was Leda's adventure, and she paid every penny for it. They asked the pit boss for directions, and he pointed down the stern and up at the ceiling, "Head for the flying whale." The gigantic inflatable creature he pointed to was bigger than a school bus. It looked like a tiny goldfish from where they were standing.

At the apex of the ship's courtyard, the terraces converge into a waterfall of cantilevered balconies. Dangling gardens of giant foliage intermingle with rippling curtains of falling water. The Captain's Table was perched at the top, hosting the best view of The Silver Pegasus. Dennis explained as the white whale grew, "The Pegasus flies under the flag of Libertalia. You can do or get just about anything up here." Leda asked him, "Libertalia? Where's that?" Blueman answered, "It's a region of Madagascar corporately owned by pirates." Dennis added, "The UAE is allowing The Silver Pegasus to use its airspace for the summer." Blueman remarked, "The only thing keeping the Pegasus afloat is extravagance." Leda thought Blueman was talking about her until Dennis explained, "Despite the UAE's war against pirates, the Pegasus gets a pass because of its popularity. How do you close down a casino like this?" Blueman nodded, "Pirates will always be smarter than bureaucrats."

The whale graced the chamber with its calligraphy. Like a ballerina, it beckoned itself to the crystal roof to breathe. Her belly pulsed as she sipped ripples of light from the ceiling. Leda was mesmerized until Dennis whispered trivia into her ear, "It's not a whale. It's a dugong. It's sort of like a manatee with a fishtail. Very exotic. Very rare. Very magical."

The Captain's Table was a ritual experience where every dish was unique. The restaurant centers around a red conveyor belt. Its winding path of finely plated cuisine emerges from the kitchen and surrounds the entire room. Its journey ends in the center, where an incinerator's fiery mouth burns every unclaimed plate. The experience is divine because every bite is fleeting, and no two dishes are alike.

Blueman was in the restroom zipping his pants when a hand landed on his shoulder and said, "Jonathan? I thought that was you." Blueman felt exposed when he heard that name. He turned to his accuser and answered him," Hi, Philip." Blueman noticed Dennis lingering at the sink. Dennis wasn't washing his hands. He seemed to think looking through the reflection made him invisible. Blueman found Dennis in the mirror and scolded him like a child, "Do you mind?" After Dennis left the bathroom, Philip asked, "Who is that?" Blueman answered, "A patient." Philip whispered with concern, "What kind of patient?" Blueman answered, "The kind that tries mine." Philip replied, "Of all the places I'd see you, this has gotta be the gold standard. Sally is going to flip! How long are you aboard?" Blueman ignored the question, "Sally, is here with you?" He answered, "Trip of a lifetime! What are the odds we'd find you?!"

Blueman broke out of the restroom like a thoroughbred to find Leda. It was too late. Sally had already touched her shoulder and said, "Leda?" Leda answered, "Yes. My name is Leda. Do I know you?" Sally was staring at a ghost and apologized, "You couldn't. That wouldn't be possible." Sally tried to acknowledge Blueman's arrival, but her mouth had already caved. Philip came out of the bathroom to join them.

He saw Leda's face with amazement and said, "Leda?" Blueman said to everyone but Dennis, "I think we should sit down."

The hostess said, "We have a table at the incinerator?" Dennis looked at everyone excitedly, "Best seat in the house." Dennis explained, "You'd think it'd be the worst, right? The end of the line is what everyone rejected from the kitchen. But watching things burn in a pillar of fire is simply mesmerizing." Blueman told Dennis, "This is family time, Dennis. I need some time alone with my daughter." Sally spat at Blueman, "Daughter?" Dennis pointed accusingly, "I knew it." Sally looked at Dennis, "Who the hell are you?" Dennis tried to defend himself, "I'm the ship's dentist." Philip told Dennis, "Sure you are, pal. Look, I hope you get better someday. I do. Now get lost." Sally asked Leda, "What are you, like, twelve?" Leda replied, "What are you, like, jealous?" Philip and Blueman met eyes like old times, watching sisters fight.

The four of them sat down. Sally asked Leda as politely as she could, "Who told you your name was Leda?" Blueman tried to slow them down, but Leda responded, "No one told me. That's my name. Leda." Philip looked at Blueman, "You cloned your wife?" Sally asked Blueman, "Does she know?" Sally didn't wait for a response. She looked at Leda, "Do you know?" Leda sat up in her chair defensively and lied, "Maybe?" Sally was astonished by the mannerisms and resemblance. She couldn't help but cry as she looked at Blueman and started to shake like a volcano, "You. You cloned my dead sister?" Blueman could understand Sally's shock, but he didn't care. Blueman felt he owed something to Leda, so he turned to her clone and said, "I'm sorry."

Leda scanned Blueman's face, inspecting every pore for insincerity. She didn't find it. She held his cheeks like a baby and told him she understood. The dugong crested the surface to drink as the ceiling rippled with sparkles. Leda understood who she was for the first time and took a deep breath. She realized all the ghosts Leda had been carrying didn't belong to her. They belonged to Blueman, and she was finally free. A slice of cheesecake grazing peacefully on a valley of shredded mint slipped by and entered the fire in a dramatic whoosh. Its delicate glass barge disappeared in a firework of vapor, capturing the moment's spectroscopy.

Leda flew home curled up in a ball on Blueman's lap. Both of them had crashed from different climaxes. Both of them owned new obligations to the museum. Blueman felt peace as he watched the carpet of desert harden into the mountains of Africa. The first Homo sapiens gazed at the same Mount Kilimanjaro he saw now out his window. Its shape hasn't budged, but its color sure did. Blueman pictured the way humanity's ancestors rendered its peak.

Aristotle described rainbows as having three colors, none of them being blue. The common description of a tri-colored rainbow was common as late as the 17th century. The Post-diluvian eye could only render red, yellow, and green. Their retina lacked the resolution for things as fancy as orange or purple. As Leda said, only a few are fortunate enough to see it from up here.

It was dark when Blueman returned to the shamba. He dragged himself across the courtyard towards the pool house. He smelled Linus' aura rushing down the fire escape to catch up to him. Linus did a terrible job of small talk as he followed Blueman to his front door, "How was your trip?" Blueman didn't answer. He unlocked the door, and Linus came inside uninvited. Blueman placed his bag on the same chair where it spent most of its life. He waited for Linus to speak and said, "What do you want?" Linus tried to act insulted, "I want an answer." Blueman's mind was still in Dubai, "Answer? To what?" Linus' frustration spiked, and he snapped, "Good lord, Blueman. I'm talking about the serum. I want in the Black-Eye Club."

Blueman answered Linus, "Is that all?" Linus didn't move. Blueman didn't appreciate Linus' determination and told him, "Focus on your chair dryer and leave the demon watching to more qualified people." Linus pushed back," Chair dryer?" Linus was angry now, "Oh, is that supposed to be funny? Dr. Frankenstein plays house with epileptic orphans but somehow decides who's qualified to see. You're a menace, Blueman! And a psychopath." Linus stormed out of the threshold, and Blueman closed the door.

Linus' aura stomped across the courtyard like a dust devil of bitterness and self-hatred. Blueman liked Linus, but people never appreciated the medicine from his rejection. Linus lacks the depth necessary to see his demons, and his reaction proves it to Blueman. It wasn't his fault. Linus' life had been too soft, and Blueman knew the serum would melt the plastic coating holding it in place. Everyone assumes they're not crazy. And this is what makes the serum so hard to take. Being sane isn't a good thing when society has normalized denial. Sure, everyone gets to feel sane, but only at the cost of mass psychosis.

CHAPTER SIXTEEN
Cobalt

Sally's face at the casino was a homecoming for Blueman. Hearing his name after all this time was a punch in the gut. He raped her family line by taking her sister's genes without consent. Blueman knew it was wrong and expected to pay for his actions. He hoped to, at least. The ability to see Leda again was the only reality Blueman could survive.

Before he knew her, Blueman's name was Jonathan Bloom. Jonathan met her on campus, where he finished his medical degree. She was a permanent volunteer in a long-term clinical trial where her unique genetics were considered an asset. Leda was a hermaphrodite. The amplification of two competing fertility systems demonstrated itself in Leda's environment through audible hallucinations and shadowy figures appearing in the room. Leda was diagnosed schizophrenic, but the truth was more complicated.

The couple fell in love. Jonathan stabilized Leda which gave him a bigger purpose. He asked her to marry him, but Leda refused. It was a shock when they found out about the pregnancy. Everyone, including them, suspected Jonathan was the father. Leda's clinical trial required Jonathan to confirm his paternity. He submitted a sample, but the results were inconclusive. No one considered the possibility that Leda could have been the father but she was.

Leda died in a miscarriage. The autopsy said it was an aneurysm in the abdominal aorta. No one knew that Jonathan had found the body first. The coroner's report revealed the corpse was tampered with post-mortem. Leda's uterus had been opened and scraped clean with a spatula. Leda's biology made her a headline for wild speculation.

Jonathan Bloom would soon disappear. His whereabouts were of little concern to anyone. Months later, a man calling himself "Blueman" crawled into a bar in South Africa, trying to negotiate a surrogate. After much searching, Blueman discovered the museum and its ties to the orphanage. They agreed to share a mutual interest in Leda's reboot, and Blueman's life made a turn.

CHAPTER SEVENTEEN

Marco

Argentina would finally outlaw human cloning in 1997, but they have a long history of human trafficking. Over three hundred facilities have been exposed in a human rights court, and its missing persons database sits in the tens of thousands. The first human clone farms were started here during WW2, and no one complained. While the rest of the world viewed human cloning as immoral, Argentina was perfecting a cottage industry.

The biggest challenge facing human cloning is not the technology. It's the lobbying. Argentina wants a future where corporations farm their own children, and many of their clients have already seen the benefits of workers with a predisposed genetic loyalty to their board.

Polo superstar Tito Cambiaso is a millionaire supermodel and fashion tycoon. He made world headlines for riding six cloned ponies in a polo championship. What people don't know is Tito himself is a clone. His genetic line was converted into a shell corporation in 1986 and is managed by a private group of investors. Tito's official life is a conglomeration of multiple body doubles. His bloodline is managed like royalty, where every decision is for the family. Tito is the third

Cambiaso to serve as CEO and the latest celebrity to purchase a membership in the Black-Eye Club.

Blueman and Sawa arrived at the Cambiaso estate in Buenos Aires at sunset. A man escorted them through the house into the rear courtyard overlooking the gardens. Blueman was noticeably surprised to see Dr. Solomon. Tito and Blueman shook hands while Dr. Solomon remained seated. Solomon greeted Blueman warmly, saying, "I hope you don't mind the company. Tito and I have a shared interest in his future, and what you offer is a radical upgrade to a significant investment of mine." Tito explained, "Dr. Solomon convinced me of your expertise. Without his confidence, you would not be here." Blueman assured them, "This is fate. You could not have timed this better as I have someone I'd like you to meet. This is Sawa. He will be your guide during the installation ceremony." A woman emerged from the house to announce el cena on the patio.

Over dinner, Blueman was especially talkative, "Every linear cosmology delegates the body's most complicated anatomy to a prolonged mutation of chance. We bite our tail, insisting evolution explains what we see when it can't." Solomon grinned, "So what explains it?" Blueman replied, "Genetic artificial intelligence from the ancient future." Tito knew enough English to ask, "What is the ancient future?" Blueman responded, "A culture and technology more advanced than we are today but existing in the ancient past."

Blueman explained, "Our cells have a universal programming language communicating through their ion channels. This network is self-organizing and modular. We can use electricity to reassign cells to be anything the body wants. You want an eye on your back; all it takes is to give a cell the right voltage. If this new eye is near the spine, its cells will begin to broadcast their data to the spinal cord. The brain will receive its information and interact with it using the laws of supply and demand. It's an open-source chemical economy where everything is exchanged on an open market. This design is far more profound than linear evolution rolling itself out in a game of chance."

Tito was bored. He turned to Sawa, "They tell me you see Hades naturally?" Sawa did not understand, so Blueman helped him, "You see, Jahanamu." Sawa nodded shyly. Blueman said, "People like Sawa have always seen Hades. They don't know what it's like not to see it. Tito asked Sawa, "You must think I am crazy to want to see like you, no?" Sawa nodded again shyly, and the men laughed as they praised him for his honesty.

Blueman said, "Albinism is not a singular monocle into this hidden world. The microscope sees the tiny. The telescope sees the large. The amygdala sees the horrid. Hades is not a new frontier. It's the oldest we've ever known, and the serum shows it to you." Tito asked, "Has Sawa taken the serum?" Blueman answered, "It is not necessary. What the serum does to you and me happens in Sawa naturally. All Sawa needed was practice enduring the heat of unfiltered reality."

Solomon noted, "Sawa is a Necromancer." Blueman concurred, "Yes. I suppose he is." Tito wondered, "Necromancy?" Solomon replied, "The oldest form of soothsayer; used and quoted extensively in Biblical times. Jesus was a necromancer." Tito raised his eyebrows in jest, "Watch your tongue, friend. People love Jesus." Solomon responded, "And so they should. I make no judgments upon the savior of man. Quite the opposite. Most of the miracles performed by Jesus were necromancy." Blueman agreed, "The blind man at the well." Tito asked, "How does curing a blind man count as necromancy?" Blueman asked Tito, "Does a blind man truly suffer from thirst as he perches himself in front of the busiest well in the village?" Solomon chuckled as

Tito contemplated. Blueman continued, "Jesus saw the blind man possessed by a lie and cured him. The man's demon was lying to the public, and Jesus exorcised it. He cured the blind man by sticking mud in his eye to show him his dirty vision." Solomon told Tito, "Necromancy is the gift of seeing what no one wants to see. In Jesus' case, it was a society where no one can trust each other." Blueman agreed, "One of the reasons Sawa is treated so harshly is people can feel his witness. It cuts through their haze like a laser. Shamans are powerful in Africa because they wield the power of transparency." Tito asked Sawa, "You see like Jesus?" Sawa shook his head and goofed, "No, I see like Sawa."

Blueman said to Tito, "You will see like the Shaman. Sawa is here to help. But, as you have been warned numerous times, there is no anti-serum. A portion of your brain will carry the rabies virus for the rest of your life. Once the virus is installed, there is no coming back." Tito would not be deterred and smirked, "Yes, Blueman. You're like a broken record." Blueman said, "I mean no disrespect. I know of no finer caliber candidate than yourself. Hades is hidden for a reason. It can be terrifying to behold everyone's urges conglomerated in a jet stream of denial, cannibalism, and possession."

Blueman strapped Tito into the chair and brought Sawa to his side. Tito joked, "There's my white rabbit." Sawa said nothing to Tito. He felt sorry for him, not because of the serum but because he was a clone. Sawa saw how fragmented Tito had become in his hive. The serum would reveal this, and it would be challenging to face. Sawa believed that even if this killed Tito, he deserved to know who he was.

Blueman immobilized cranial nerves three and seven with lidocaine. The serum came in two parts. The first injection flooded Tito's epithelial layer with melanin, causing Tito's eye to darken in a milky black ink. The second injection released Blueman's rabies into the eye. The charged blue plasma reacts to the melanin and retreats up the optic nerve. It gathers along the hippocampus and slowly disables the amygdala's signal to secrete melanin. As long as the eye remains black, the rabies remains alive. This makes the amygdala open its curtain for everything to come through.

Blueman asked Sawa to kill the lights while they waited for the serum to activate. Solomon asked Blueman, "Is he blind now in his right eye?" Blueman answered, "No, he fully hallucinates in his right eye. He is blind in the left eye. All of the spatial data Tito uses as an athlete doesn't come from his vision. Vision is too slow. His eyes work because the brain can holograph data into them and hallucinate. Like Sawa, it will take Tito several months to adjust, but I am confident he will excel quickly."

Tito regained feeling in his face and began to complain about the discomfort. Blueman seemed pleased with the results and unstrapped Tito's head. Tito asked to see a mirror and was unimpressed, "I see me." Blueman replied, "Wait for it." Tito was unconvinced until he made eye contact with Sawa. He jumped as if electrocuted by a snake. He flexed every muscle under the restraints. Sawa got closer, and Tito winced. His eyes were closed to protect himself. He was terrified as hives of sweat were gushing out of his pores.

Blueman calmed him, "Relax, Tito. Sawa lit your fuse, is all. You are seeing through the eyes of the shaman now. Sawa sees this every moment of every day. Don't look at me; look at Sawa. I know it burns, but he will regulate you." Tito crawled into Sawa's eyes and begged for mercy. Blueman and Solomon stepped outside to give them privacy. Tito remained strapped to the chair for everyone's safety. The two men went out on the veranda and watched the stars. Solomon asked him, "Tell me. Is this your first time giving serum to a clone?" Blueman answered without thinking, "I guess so." It had never occurred to Blueman, so he asked, "Why do you ask?" Solomon shrugged, "Why does anyone ask questions?"

Solomon and Blueman returned to a cloudy room of angst. Sawa had stepped back from Tito and told Blueman, "Something is wrong. I do not know what to do." The gurney was quaking from Tito's convulsions. He was bucking himself off the ground like a horse. Blueman jumped on top of him, but Tito was too strong. Tito saw Solomon in the doorway and cursed him, "You! El Diablo! You did this to us!" Tito popped one of the rivets securing his wrist and grabbed Blueman by the throat. Blueman felt his life was over until Tito pleaded, "You have to kill me. Promise me you will kill every one of us." Tito motioned to Solomon. Before he could speak, Tito's face went limp. Blueman gasped and coughed as he peeled his neck out of the clutches of the unconscious madman. Solomon removed a ring and placed it in his vest pocket. Blueman still had his eyes on Tito, ensuring he wasn't moving. Solomon assured him, "You are safe now. Tito is fine. He needs some time to reflect on what he saw." Tito was taken to his room to recover from the experience.

Blueman and Solomon spent the evening on the terrace watching the stars roll out of the water. Blueman asked, "You knew this would happen, right?" Solomon nodded, "Yes, I did." Blueman was angry, "Is this your way of securing my slavery?" Solomon replied, "Slavery? Freedom? Those are funny notions. I'm a bit surprised you haven't become a chemical determinist by now. Man's fate is written in his chemicals, and nothing he does is free from their intimidation. But I did not come to intimidate you, Blueman. I came to show you I am your superior so you would believe me. I came to stop you. The serum is a distraction. I have something you have been looking for since she died. We can both have what we want if you work with me."

Solomon didn't need to say her name. Blueman felt the betrayal from his thoughts. His body language and face gave everything away to someone like Solomon. Blueman tried to argue, "You're lying. You promise things you can't deliver." Solomon replied, "I will never lie. I do not need to debase myself. Nor do I need your serum to see your field. Let's be plain. You're not bringing her back. Leda has already proven that. She wanted Tombo, not you." Blueman snarled, "That's the hormones." Solomon snickered, "Look at you. Do you think this technology makes you invisible? Just because you found Hades doesn't mean you own the place or can see it any deeper than I do." Blueman was undeterred, "Are you implying my serum is too weak?" Solomon replied calmly, "I lack the poverty to imply, Mr Blueman. It seems odd you expect everyone but you to drink the truth. Deep down, you know the world is not ready for your serum."

Blueman still had some fight, "But Tito is a clone, and the serum is too much for them. That's a tiny community." Solomon laughed, "Man has been cloning for longer than you think. Haven't you ever wondered why the XY chromosome is so small and convenient to work with? Haven't you wondered why it comes with a radioactive dye allowing you to read a sequence from the comforts of a microscope?" Blueman agreed, "Chromosome twenty-three is an oddity. Most DNA requires more code to determine gender. It's hard-coded millions of times throughout the sequence." Solomon agreed, "But not man. Why does man have this access panel of chromosomes where traits like gender, hair and eye color, height, and even metabolic rate can be assigned so conveniently?" Blueman considered the implication, "So you're saying there are more clones?"

Solomon turned to Sawa, "Sawa? May we have some privacy, please." Sawa left the pair alone, and Solomon said, "What if it were possible for you to pay for your sin and see her again, too? Would that interest you?" Blueman started to protest, but Solomon stopped him, "Blueman, before you doubt my sincerity, please remember I can see you. I am offering you a contract to work directly with me, and as a bonus, I can introduce you to the missing piece you need to find Leda."

Blueman wondered if this was a dream and if Solomon was even human. The thought was so uncomfortable he found himself angry, "If you know so much more about cloning than I do, why do you need me? Why haven't you told me any of this sooner? Why waste both of our time if my work is so elementary?" Solomon balked respectfully, "Elementary is where we are in the field of cloning, and you are a maestro at what you do. But understand, I don't need you, Blueman. Humanity needs you. You are helping humanity become more open to cloning, and if we are going to survive the next deluge, we will need clones to do it." Blueman was overloaded and angry because deep down, even without the serum, he could sense Solomon was sincere.

Tito was put down by his corporation in an emergency vote forty minutes after he was declared incapacitated. A loophole in the bylaws meant his condition disqualified him from voting. It was a fast and unanimous decision to terminate him. The house manager appeared at breakfast and informed them that Mr. Cambiaso would not be entertaining guests that day. Blueman was confused, "I must see Mr. Cambiaso before I go. I need to assess his reaction." The house manager did not oblige Blueman's intensity. He told them a transport was waiting to take them back to the airport. Solomon rose politely and said to the house manager, "Inform Mr Cambiaso how grateful we are for the visit, and I look forward to seeing him next month."

CHAPTER EIGHTEEN

Contract

Solomon and Blueman shared the plane to Dubai, which gave Blueman a chance to think. He poured them a drink from the bar as Solomon answered Blueman's question, "Your world resets itself every 6000-12000 years, and the museum is here to recolonize after the collapse." Blueman chided, "Reset. What's like Noah's Ark?" Solomon nodded, "Yes. The Epic of Gilgamesh is a flood story. The Aztecs have a flood story. Most of the early tribes in America have one, too. Every quarter in the great year seems to compost civilization in a fallow period. Blueman asked, "Great year?" Solomon replied, "Yes. The celestial clock repeats itself every 26,000 years. Each era in the great year is a movement through the zodiac, lasting every 2,166 years. These changes are humanity's winter. There's nothing exact or predictable about it. There is no countdown or doomsday clock we can watch."

Blueman realized he didn't care about civilization and hadn't for a long time. His loss had separated him from society. This new insight gave him a better look at the museum and why everything was urgent. Solomon seemed to be reading his mind when he said, "If the museum fails to preserve humanity, civilization is forced to start over from the beginning and lose 200,000 years of progress." Blueman was shocked, "Jesus! How many floods have you guys survived?" Solomon answered, "This will be Ark number five. But there have been too many to count because we lack the tools to see that far back in time. I suspect we have been doing this for millions of years. We only know what has been recorded in the Great Hall, and most of those records melted."

Blueman asked, "Why haven't I heard this before? Why isn't everyone talking about this?" Solomon chuckled, "You should know. Denial. Fear. Regret. Shock. Society does not want to embrace the idea that everything they built could be destroyed. None of this is hidden information. People refuse to admit it. The footprints are there, but modern man insists these resets are simply dynasties stacked on top of each other. Everything known has to fit inside a single timeline we call history. This is how you apply the scientific method."

Blueman was stunned as he realized, "So I guess this explains how the museum managed to find a pristine tribe of aborigines?" Solomon laughed, "See? Even you couldn't see the truth at first." Blueman was stunned. "But how?" Solomon replied. "We have never seen real estate on any map. Convincing the world everything has been discovered is easier than you think. The Great Hall left us a manual on raising a human crop the fastest way possible. This is our great work and the only driving factor for anyone who sees what's happening and wants to find a way out." Blueman asked him, "Out? How does one get out?" Solomon replied, "If I knew that Blueman, I wouldn't be here. All these questions have answers in Antarctica, where you can read the writing yourself."

Blueman said, "So you have a library in Antarctica?" Solomon replied, "The Great Hall is where this is documented. Every reset has left a record of what they did to preserve humanity." Blueman sat back in his seat as a rushing jolt of invigoration came into him. Ancient memories were connecting for the first time. It reminded him of what it felt like to be Jonathan.

Blueman looked out the window as the jet breached the coast of South Africa. He remembered smuggling the fertilized eggs of the woman he loved through airport security. He had been chasing a ghost for seventeen years and still hadn't found her. After some time, he asked Solomon, "Are we in hell?" Solomon seemed surprised, "I don't follow?" Blueman was just as confused, "Something Leda told me. She's convinced this place is Hades." Solomon nodded and made a sound, "Hard to imagine someone like Leda living the life she did and not thinking this place was hell." Blueman said nothing.

Solomon contemplated what he would say next, "Mythology is a wonderful oracle. Hades is both a place and a man. He rules the underworld with his wife, Persephone. Persephone embodies the concept of regenerative wisdom in corn and other grains. These are ancient artifacts from ancient civilizations much more advanced than yours. Once you see this place completely, it becomes easy to recognize man's fruits. Apples, oranges, figs, olives, pears, and, of course, pomegranates. These were genetic gifts made by ancient man when people did more than fly around in aluminum chariots at 40,000 feet."

Blueman considered the genetics of fruit, "A seed is the perfect form of compression. But how do you install wisdom through a stomach? That can't work. How do the genes get from the fruit into the DNA of the person who ate it?" Solomon answered," Flavor is wisdom's activation. When you taste something, its ancient memory is activated. This is why food tastes good. Salt is a memory we have forgotten. Pepper is a memory we already know. No DNA is transferred when a man eats fruit. Instead, the flavor activates an engram hardcoded in the motor cortex, and the engram decompresses the memory and prints its flavor to the tongue. The more critical the memory, the better its flavor tends to be. "

Blueman's mind was blown, "So every taste I have is just a memory of something my ancestor stored?" Solomon nodded, "It goes even deeper. Ancient man's fingerprints are inside your anatomy right now. A brain space is hidden inside the cerebellum, and the museum has a way to read and write into its time capsule."

Blueman sank into his chair and connected the dots. Solomon confirmed, "Yes. You're getting it now. But it's so much more. Our love of flowers. Our fear of cilantro. These daemons, as you call them, are decompressed through the flavor palette." Blueman continued, "I suppose that's how we got our language center, too?" Solomon nodded, "Indeed. It's the oldest code we know."

Solomon said, "This technique is tricky because we can only install engrams in the primitive brain. They must survive dormant for thousands of years until the species demonstrates sapience. By then, the constellations have changed, and your symbolism has shifted. It's a science of mythology as much as genetics." Blueman interrupted in a revelation, "So we taste constellations?" Solomon chuckled, "Precisely. The primal man was rewarded with dopamine every time he recognized the shape of Orion. He follows This synaptic trail, naturally unlocking ancient flavors along the way, leading him like an animal outside the cave before he drowns all over again. The cerebellum is the only place to plant these kinds of seeds."

Blueman pondered, "It's remarkable anthropologists don't see these clues." Solomon teased Blueman, "Well, you didn't catch them either. Mythology is what happens to man. Ancient history is what he tells himself to feel better. This is why the museum's work is so important."

Blueman kept his gaze out the window as they flew over the northern range of mountains known as the barrier of spears. He asked Solomon, "Just how old is this place anyway?" Solomon replied, "Sign the contract, Blueman, and you will have access to information even I haven't had time to read. I know that our realm inhales and expels recollection every 6,000 years, give or take a few. Mystery and omniscience are two extremes of this spectrum. This place isn't created and destroyed so much as it is forgotten and remembered." Blueman thought about the Bible and realized artificial insemination was an immaculate conception with the right clinic. He remarked, "Funny. I never expected someone like you would bring me to religion." Solomon laughed, "If you only knew the irony."

Blueman noted, "Tito called you the devil. He wanted me to kill all of his clones. He said you tricked him." Solomon agreed with Tito's observations, "Yes. Many Tito have wanted to die since we met. This happens a lot with clones." Blueman asked, "So why don't you help him?" Solomon nodded again, agreeing, "I have and still am. Tito's sovereignty is controlled by a board. I am their chairperson. This is a title with very little power. Tito blames me because the moment one of him dethrones me, the rest can fight for who gets to be in charge." Blueman seemed to understand and asked, "Which Tito do you honor?" Solomon welcomed his empathy, saying, "It would be murder. Don't think I haven't considered it. Every month, I call for a vote, but there is always one of him who has changed his mind or a new objection from someone who is not quite ready to go. I think they each believe all of them will commit suicide except one. They constantly plot against each other while currying favor with each other's court. I agree with you when you say the Cambiasos are living in hell. But what can I do without violating the will of a free man who chose to clone himself?"

Blueman spent the next few hours reading Solomon's contract. He turned to page six and read the sixth paragraph. The last sentence read as follows, "All employees of the museum who die on premises lose the rights to their carcass." Blueman noticed this was a policy similar to the ones his crew signed in Australia, but he never considered it for himself. His head was exploding from the things that waited for him after his signature. The old Blueman might have refused on principle, but he considered what he had done to Leda and decided this clause agreed with him. Blueman signed the contract as "Jonathan Bloom" and returned it to Solomon, saying, "That's my legal name." Solomon nodded and said, "Yes, I know." The two men shook hands and charted their next move. Blueman would return to the shamba, collect his work, and fly to Antarctica, where he would see everything.

CHAPTER NINETEEN

Centaur

The identical Finns found Linus with his back turned, closing the doors to his study. He turned to see them and was startled enough to yelp noticeably. Linus' face blushed from embarrassment as he tried to explain, "Holy cow, you scared me! I don't mean you scared me, of course. I just mean anyone standing there like you were just now would have scared me." Linus swallowed. The Finns were motionless in their contempt and spoke in two-part harmony, "Buddy wants you in the lab." Linus agreed to the summons, "Yes. I will do that. I need a moment alone, though. Not from you, two, I mean. Just a moment." Linus stopped hyperventilating once they left the house.

Buddy showed Linus the monitor in the lab and said, "Leda's eggs can't be fertilized in vitro. We have to do this in the womb, like our horses." Linus made a face, so Buddy assured him," I know she's not a horse, but see for yourself. The sperm isn't even trying. They're swimming right past the egg." Linus noticed it, too. Buddy said, "I told Blueman this was a possibility." Linus asked Buddy, "So what do you want me to do?" Buddy replied, "You might be able to get Leda's sperm in the mood." Linus asked, "Sperm? I thought you

wanted her eggs?" Buddy answered, "We have all the eggs we
need. Now we need the sperm." Linus knew about Leda, but
he had never considered this side of her. Buddy asked him,
"Your chair works on men, right?" Linus answered
defensively, "I don't know. Probably." Buddy lowered his
head a few degrees, "Linus?" Buddy asked again, "You're
telling me you've never tried your orgasm chair?" Linus
realized his dignity was pointless. He snatched the container
from Buddy's hand and said, "Yes, it works fine. "

Linus found Leda in the kitchen washing a tea cup. Leda
teased him about a particularly loud session with Rose the
day prior, saying, "Your chair makes a lot of noise." Linus
confessed, "Yeah. I've been told." Leda circled her target like a
shark, "I wonder if it could help me?" Linus laughed and
ended her charade, "I guess Buddy told you what we need?"
Leda giggled, "Shall I use this cup, or do you have something
better in mind?" Linus found solace in her vulgarity. She
brought a radical honesty he felt safe around. He tried to
escort Leda through the house, but she knew the place better
than he did. This was her first home. When they got to his
door, she showed him how it sticks. There wasn't a single
moment that Linus was in charge, but all that changed when
she sat in his chair.

Linus ruined the vibe by unwrapping the specimen jar
from its plastic and placing it on a table. His language was
sterile as he asked Leda, "How would you prefer to stimulate
your, uh, your member?" She answered defensively, "Let me
help. It's called a penis. And it doesn't work. It never has.
What's next, Linus? What's your next stupid question?" Linus
swallowed several times and let his intuition take over. He
removed the specimen cup from the table and buried his
awareness in the chair's control panel. He initiated a pulse
aimed at the sacrum at twenty hertz. He slowed his voice to a
crawl and asked Leda, "Is that comfortable?" She sat back and

nodded. Linus' confidence rose in the saddle as he watched her relax. The sound of his voice hung Leda's boundaries on the bed like a robe. Every other second, a tickle from the sixty-hertz sweep surprised her. Each tone felt like the teeth of a rubber comb pulling stones to the surface. Linus launched his sonic clouds at the ceiling so their music fell like rain on her face. Like a conductor, he played his music for her and said, "We can go deeper. "

For once, Leda let go. She felt the render of her childhood play in her veins. People at the orphanage were triggered by Leda. They reacted harshly when they discovered her condition. They teased her and called her names. Some of the older children had threatened to operate with scissors. She wanted them to fix her, but all they ever did was make her bleed. The musk from Leda's fear was an aphrodisiac to any predator. She sweats the power of infinity. This is the fountain of youth for anyone afraid to die.

Linus watched her body convulse as he twisted the dials like a lifeline. She relived these events in her body while the constellations exploded in her mind. Linus didn't need to say a word. He told himself everything Leda needed was in her bones. Leda said, "Not everything." It took Linus a few moments to realize she was talking to him. He pushed the headphones from his skull and asked, "What do you mean?" Leda replied, "You thought everything I needed came from my bones, but that's not true. Not everything." Linus felt as stunned as he was violated, "Did you just read my mind?" Leda nodded calmly. Linus tested her by thinking, "What about now?" She smiled as if they were flirting. Linus thought, "Can I read your mind?" Leda answered with her mouth, "Only when it's pretty. Otherwise, you'll curse it all to Hades and never see me."

Linus used his words, "Hades?" Leda nodded, saying, "Hell. Hades. The underworld. The unseen realm. This is it,

Linus. It's all around you, but you can't see it. Not yet. I can sense you feel it, though. I can sense this is why you decided to come to Africa. Doesn't it feel like we're in Hell?" Linus answered, "No." Leda chuckled, "Exactly. Only in Hell would people swear they weren't there. Only in hell would people eat each other alive and call it love and commitment."

Leda leaned back in the chair and continued, "You know this is Hades because the better you behave, the worse people treat you, and the more you tell the truth, the more they lie." Linus thought of Sawa and how his transparency is a curse. Leda was reassured by his thoughts, saying, "People who need lies to survive are only going to live with liars. That's why we're down here."

Linus tried to picture hell with a blue sky and a shining sun. Leda helped him, "Hell is a lake of burning fire — that sounds a lot like the sun. The underworld is blue, which sounds a lot like the sky." Linus still wasn't on board. Leda gave his thoughts some privacy and finally said. "In the underworld, everything is hidden — and that sounds a lot like denial, doesn't it, Linus?"

Linus understood Leda and repeated what she said, "If this were Hades, everyone would swear it wasn't." Unlike Linus, Leda felt comfortable being seen. She said, "That's why he wears blue." Linus was intrigued, "Who, Blueman?" Leda nodded, "He hides in the periphery so people without compassion can't see him. The blue masks his aura from their primal senses, rendering him invisible." Linus asked Leda, "You see auras?" Leda said solemnly, "We all do. I can't ignore them like you can." Leda rolled over on her side, "Most of the population are still cavemen living in the dark. If you knew what everyone was thinking, you'd know it was Hell for sure."

Linus gave Leda his eyes long enough for her to say, "You are good at what you do." Linus was embarrassed and broke her gaze to hide his apprehension, but Leda saw his aura. She could read his mind, and he thought she was a freak. Leda asked him, "Do you know what it's like to be chased by a crowd of angry villagers?" Linus replied, "No. I don't." Leda replied, "Must be nice."

Leda melted into the chair and dozed off, which was typical under this frequency. Linus programmed a long sinusoidal pattern and lay on the bed to dream. He imagined caressing Leda's beast as she lay curled up in his arms. He imagined the depth of her loneliness as a solitary species. Linus cursed himself for having apprehension about her anatomy. He closed his eyes and fell into a trance with Leda in his embrace.

Every breath betrays our feelings, and Leda's nose didn't take long to smell it. An epigenetic urge oozed out of her genes and wrapped around her spine. Smells are the joystick of the body, and Leda's back was curled in lordosis. Her eyes burst open like a minotaur released in a maze. Linus' chair was still playing its notes, and Leda was thoroughly lubricated. She found Linus on the bed and rolled him over on his back as he awoke in confusion. Her pelvis churned with lust. She ground into his saddle, asking," Help me?" The plastic cup was nowhere to be found.

Linus' body was willing, but his brain could not fathom how to proceed. Leda broke into his pants and looted his register. She finished him quickly, but the Vulcans continued to smash their hammers against her loins. She groaned and moaned in misery as he begged her to stop. Leda snorted in frustration and trounced outside to the stable.

A few minutes later, Rose came running out of the barn screaming bloody murder, "Buddy! Buddy! Leda is fucking the horses!" Leda had devolved entirely. A fit of turrets had come to the surface, and she started cursing in Swahili. One of the mares kicked Leda with the full force of her hind. Linus ran down to see Buddy and his men hogtie her with tape and roll her up in a blanket. Rose was pulling horses from the barn one by one like rescued hostages. She was mortified by what she had seen and kept repeating it over and over, but it did no good. Linus was mortified by how quickly Leda had been reduced to an animal. Buddy secured the bucking blanket with Leda thrashing inside and shouted, "Hold her!"

Linus could hear Leda grunting as he turned his body into a sandbag. Buddy ran into the tach room and opened the medicine cabinet. He filled a syringe with horse tranquilizer and ran outside, instructing the men to uncover her. They rolled her over ass-up, and Buddy stuck the needle into her rump and emptied the chamber. Leda kicked and bucked like a swordfish until she finally went offline. Her last words were slurred as she spit and cackled, "I'm a fucking monster!" They carried Leda up the fire escape and into the bathtub. Buddy saw she wasn't breathing, and he couldn't find her pulse. He gave her CPR and kept repeating, "Don't go. Don't go." But Leda didn't listen.

CHAPTER TWENTY

Eyeball

Addictions live in the pores of our skin like an energetic reef. We push their spirit in and out of our coral every time we breathe. Breath is a holy ghost swimming in the tide of the lung's caverns. This is how the will clings to a body. The more possessed the reef, the more it needs to feed. Linus was no different. His belief in his inadequacy was forged with a desire to prove others wrong. This fanatic piston of self-hate and redemption can make a man unstoppable.

Linus was armed with a pitchfork as he marched to the door of Blueman's lab. He battered his way inside with the leverage of his trident and made his way to the safe. Linus had removed the guts from his chair and attached its machinery to its walls. With a few short pulses, the safe was humming like a brass horn. Linus jiggled the tumbler until they crumbled from the heat. The safe wouldn't crack. He focused his attack on the door. He moved every resonator and raised the frequency until it began to glow. The door pried free from its gooey hinges and fell to the floor.

Inside, Linus found a human eye floating in a hermetically sealed jar and placed it on the counter. He moved aside fifty thousand dollars in cash and twelve kilos of crystal meth to reach for the two vials. Just as Leda described, one was black, and one was blue. He wrapped them in a cloth and ran out the door as the sun rose.

Blueman's jet arrived at the airfield from Argentina that afternoon. Tombo was waiting for him in the jeep and told Blueman Leda had died. Blueman didn't believe him and ordered Tombo to drive faster. If Blueman had been smart, he might have stopped to cherish Leda alive in the quantum. Before a collapse, all waves are still possible. Blueman jumped out of the jeep before it stopped and ran up the fire escape. Leda was gone. Her body curled up like a kitten in an autopsy bag labeled "Panthera Leo." Blueman surveyed the proof inside its zipper. Its contents would convince anyone with doubt that she was gone. Hades grants us the privilege of finding each other's carcass. It lets us suffer our losses properly under Hell's supervision. It's the only chance we have to prove the underworld is working.

Blueman had been here before. He came to his senses and scanned the perimeter, asking, "Where's Lyra?" Buddy answered, "Rose took her to see the rhinos." Blueman was cold as ice and asked, "You took samples?" Buddy looked at him like he was psycho, "Samples?" Blueman reminded Buddy about his job, "Leda's sperm could be in the horse." Buddy shook his head back and forth, "Are you nuts?" Blueman retorted, "Do you want to complete your contract or come with me to Dubai and answer for what happened?" Buddy considered all options apprehensively. He looked at his watch and swallowed his fate, "There's still time. I'll take care of it."

Blueman stopped Buddy, "Don't forget, Leda." Buddy retorted, "What?" Blueman explained, "We need those eggs." Buddy disagreed, "We have plenty of eggs." Blueman pressed him, "None of them are fertilized. Maybe Linus, wherever he is, did what our lab could not." Buddy was furious, "I'll sample the horse Blueman, but if you want Leda's eggs, you can climb up in there and scrape them out yourself, you sick fuck!" Blueman was primal and grabbed Buddy by his neck. He shoved his face into his eyes and cursed through his teeth, "You listen to me, Vega. I wasn't the one groping the livestock around here. The contract requires one fertilized egg. You promised me a hundred. We have zero. If we lose that egg, I will consider you a poacher, and you know what we do to poachers around here."

Lyra sat between Sawa and Rose on the vehicle's roof while the rhinos grunted at the trough. Lyra had just been told her mom died. She was more confused than sad. Leda was always going away, but Rose explained this was different. To Lyra, Leda had always been gone. Lyra understood death long before she understood life. The three sat quietly, grazing in the sunlight as Rose thought about Lyra's mom. Lyra said, "My father was a pilot." Rose had no reason to correct her.

Sawa could no longer hold his thoughts and spoke to Rose cryptically in Swahili, "She is in danger." Rose responded in English, "I know." Sawa replied in English, "But Miss Vega. You are, too." Rose asked Sawa, "What do you mean, Sawa?" Sawa handed Rose the jar and asked her, "Why does Mr Blueman have my eye?"

Rose returned to the house to hear Linus threatening to call the police. He insisted he was leaving as he frantically packed up his stuff. Buddy ordered him, "I need your DNA before you leave." Linus screamed, "What is it with you people?" Rose didn't bother to argue and called the pilot. She could hear Linus scolding Buddy in the foyer, "You people are animals." Rose yelled at Linus, "Who are you calling an animal, Linus Bardo?! You gave Leda a heart attack with that machine." Buddy returned and swabbed Linus' mouth as if he was a horse. When he got what he needed, he sealed it in a bag, placed it in his breast pocket, and punched Linus square in the face. Linus fell like a clumsy giraffe and stayed there. He caressed his eye as he heard Buddy say, "Have a nice flight."

CHAPTER TWENTY-ONE

Lyra

Blueman found Rose in the stables and asked, "Where's Lyra?" Rose replied nervously, "She is with Sawa." Rose started to shovel dung between her and Blueman. Blueman persisted, "I didn't ask who she was with. I asked, where is she?" Rose abandoned her shoveling and stepped out of the stall strong, "She's probably in the closet. You want me to drag her outside and put a saddle on her?" Blueman wouldn't relent, "I need to see her, Rose. Now!" Rose asked, "What for?" Blueman stared a hole through her. Rose acted insulted but agreed, "Fine. Come with me." Blueman followed her to the house, where she made him remove his shoes.

Rose opened the door and called out, "Lyra?" She climbed the stairs with Blueman behind her. Reaching the top, she called out again, "Lyra?" She crossed her finger over her lips and motioned to Blueman to follow her down the hall quietly. Rose pushed the door open to reveal Lyra curled up like a stone sleeping on Sawa. Sawa raised his hand in greeting, but Rose said, "Shhh." Blueman's phone chimed, and Rose rudely pushed him out of her bedroom. The text from Buddy said, "Specimen in the cooler. Looks like you had a burglar."

Rose helped Linus pack and loaded his trunk onto the jeep. Tombo drove them both to the airstrip. By the time they arrived, Linus' eye was deep purple. The trunk was loaded on the plane while Rose instructed the pilot. After the door closed, Lyra popped out of the trunk with excitement. She asked Linus, "Is this your first plane ride, too?" Rose promised Leda she would come for her right after she tended to the animals.

It would take fifteen hours to land stateside. Blueman could turn this jet around with one call and murder Linus on the runway. He was stewing in the adrenaline. His eye was throbbing, and he couldn't see a thing. Lyra had entered the cockpit by asking the pilot, "Are you my Father?" Linus tried to bury his head in his hand, but he touched his swollen eye instead. He found ice in the cooler next to the seat where he first saw Leda buckled in for takeoff. He was seated in the shadow of her ghost. Linus missed Leda, but the amount hadn't breached the surface. The pain in his eye was only the crest of that iceberg.

Linus was passed out when they received the message over the VHF asking them if they could turn around. The pilot replied, "Negative. Our PNR was two hours ago. We'll refuel at Canaveral, over." The chances of Lyra landing in Cocoa Beach on the morning of a Cape Canaveral launch would have been astounding to anyone but Lyra. She watched the rocket plume from the cockpit of their G280 bearing off her starboard bow. As the trail of smoke arched over the horizon, Lyra found her first passion.

After the jet landed, Linus' phone rang from the tarmac. It was Rose, and his hands were shaking when he answered it. Rose sounded relieved, "Blueman is gone." Linus replied, "Gone?" He listened to Rose explain as he held his posture. Rose said, "It's safe to come back." Linus jittered between the conversation and rummaging through Lyra's bag as he said into the phone, "Listen. Here's the thing." Linus unrolled the leather pouch to confirm its contents and said, "I got everything I needed from Africa." Linus rolled the vials back into their pouch and stuffed them down his pants. Rose asked, "Is this about Buddy?" Rose tried apologizing, but Linus insisted, "No, it's not that. I deserved it." Linus forgot who he was talking to and said, "He loved Leda. I did, too." Linus' head started pounding, "Listen. Lyra will be fine with Tombo. She loves to fly. I gotta go." Linus ended the call.

CHAPTER TWENTY-TWO

Poach

Hades is a fog that's missing. Its colors aren't brighter; they are more meaningful. It's like you spent your whole life drinking from a straw and suddenly took a giant gulp. You will choke if you're not careful. People think Hades is a world of demons and devils, but the truth is even scarier. What we do to each other is Hades. How we cannibalize and justify it is Hades. People here already understand why people don't want to look around.

Blueman saw Tombo's jeep returning from the airstrip and ran to meet him in the driveway. Blueman asked him, "Where's Linus?" Tombo was confused as he pointed north, "He is on the plane. Rose said you wanted him gone?" Tombo turned to Rose to confirm, but she was already in the house before Blueman could curse her. Buddy was standing guard at the front door when he heard the shot. He recognized the sound as one of his field rifles.

A bullet is a spiritual war waged at the speed of sound. It rips open a wormhole where physics and desire combine. The firing of a gun is two sounds in one. The first sound is the gunpowder exploding. This is the curse from the devil pulling the trigger. The second comes from the breaking of the sound barrier. This is the plea from an angel to make it stop.

Blueman's eye evaporated from the exit wound. His body remained erect as he turned to face his attack. Buddy saw sunlight pour through the back of Blueman's skull. Blueman found Tombo mounted on a motorcycle, holding the rifle. He noticed Sawa nearby and raised his arm to wave.

The bliss of surrender ran through Jonathan's arteries for the first time since he lost Leda. It would take a few million potassium transactions to spread the gospel inside his body. God was dead. A few moments were left before he died, but he didn't want them. Jonathan didn't need to go to Antarctica. He could pay for his sin right here in Africa.

Made in the USA
Middletown, DE
02 September 2024